FICTION

Pub Date: January 10, 2000

Price: $17.99 ($25.99 CAN)

ISBN: 0-399-23486-1

Page Count: 192

Imprint: Philomel Books

$17.99 USA
$25.99 CAN

Promise me, Jodie . . . you'll stay far far away from the Sande. It's taboo. Like I said, you're not only not welcome there— you are forbidden.

When Jodie's mother decides they are moving to Sierre Leone, Jodie feels as if her entire world is falling apart. Africa is so far away—with such strange customs and an entirely different language. How can she possibly make any friends?

But in this new place, Jodie meets Khadi, a village girl. From the moment they meet, the two are inseparable— working in the rice fields together, sharing their thoughts. Everything seems perfect to Jodie until strange things begin to happen. Most mysterious, Khadi and the other village girls begin to disappear daily. "It's Sande, Jodie. Stay away from it," her mother warns her. But Jodie wonders what this Sande—this Secret Society—is all about. Why is it so secret? For Khadi's sake, didn't she have to find out?

In an unforgettable novel that teems with authentic details of African culture and life, Cristina Kessler gracefully and heroically tackles one of the most important, most controversial issues for women of our time.

CRISTINA KESSLER—writer and photographer, first came to Africa as a Peace Corps volunteer. What is unique is that she stayed. For sixteen of the last twenty-five years, she has lived all over the continent, including Sierra Leone, where *No Condition is Permanent* takes place. Armed with a "little portable typewriter" and her "trusty journal," Cristina began her writing career there, where, like *No Condition*'s Jodie and her mother, she never had running water, rarely had electricity, and always had snakes. Most of the events found in the book are based on her experiences in Sierra Leone.

Cristina currently resides in Mali with her husband, Joe. In addition to *No Condition is Permanent*, her first novel, she has also written *One Night: a story from the desert*, a picture book illustrated by Ian Schoenherr.

Jacket art © 2000 by Raul Colon
Reinforced Binding

P H I L O M E L   B O O K S
a division of
Penguin Putnam Books for Young Readers
345 Hudson Street
New York, NY 10014

0001
http://www.penguinputnam.com

no condition is
permanent

ART TK

no condition is permanent

cristina kessler

Philomel Books • New York

Patricia Lee Gauch, editor

Copyright © 2000 by Cristina Kessler. All rights reserved. This book, or
parts thereof, may not be reproduced in any form without permission in
writing from the publisher
PHILOMEL BOOKS,
a division of Penguin Putnam Books for Young Readers,
345 Hudson Street, New York, NY 10014.
Philomel Books, Reg. U.S. Pat & Tm. Off.
Published simultaneously in Canada.
Printed in the United States of America.
Book design by Semadar Megged
The text is set in 11.5 – point Berling
Library of Congress Cataloging-in-Publication Data
Kessler, Cristina.
No condition is permanent / Cristina Kessler.
p. cm.
SUMMARY: When shy fourteen-year-old Jodie accompanies her anthro-
pologist mother to live in Sierra Leone, she befriends a local girl but
encounters a cultural divide that cannot be crossed.
[1. Sierra Leone—Fiction. 2. Female circumcision—Fiction.
3. Friendship—Fiction.] I. Title.
PZ7.K4824 No 2000 [Fic]—dc21 99-27265 CIP
ISBN 0-399-23486-1
1 3 5 7 9 10 8 6 4 2
First Impression

Y Y Y Y Y

To Joe and Paulette,
Valerie,
Ma Kargbo
and Patti,

Ah say tank ya pas words.
Ah beg, let there be peace in Sierra Leone jus now.

Ɏ Ɏ Ɏ Ɏ Ɏ

Krio is one of the official languages of Sierra Leone. It's a fun language that has a rhythmic sound when spoken well. The key pronunciations are listed below, and by usingthese sounds all words can be easily pronounced.

A sounds like AH, as in blah.
E sounds like A, as in day.
I sounds like E, as in we.
O is O, as in oh.
U is U, as in you.
"Ow di go de go?" is pronounced *Aww dee go day go?* It means "How are things? What's new?"
If you play with the sounds as they appear you should be speaking some Krio by the time you finish the book! Have fun!

no condition is
permanent

first words

As they talked, I wound my way through the market. Three women dressed in matching gowns and headties the color of fire trucks danced to a drum played by a fourth friend. Kids ran between legs, chasing chickens and each other, and goats, tied to trees, bleated unhappily. Two men laughed loudly, slapping hands high and low in a private joke, while the bread man walked through the crowd shouting out "Hot Bread! Too too fresh."

I wandered past a long row of onions and chili peppers, then got stuck in a crowd that was not moving. Standing in front of a stall of festering meat and dried fish, flies landed on my arms. I flailed at them like someone flagging down a car, until I noticed a strange silence. All the jabber and music and screaming and laughter had stopped, as if someone had turned off a noise tap.

In the silence the smell of rotting meat got worse, sending out a stink strong enough to scorch paint. The butcher had stopped his tired swipes with his fly whisk as he stared to his left.

That's when I saw her.

The top of her head must have reached my shoulder, with a face older than time. Her black dress and cape, cinched tightly around her circular waist by a belt of snake skin, looked slightly faded against her deep black skin. A very big python had provided her belt.

A black cloth covered her head, also cinched tight with a snakeskin headband. Our eyes met as she stalked toward me, and I felt locked into her stare. Her eyes glinted in the sun. Sunken into her dry wrinkled skin, they looked just like snake eyes.

I wanted to look away, but I couldn't. As she reached me, she deliberately lifted a small bag attached to her wrist and pointed it at me. Faded green, the snakeskin looked like an old dried mamba. Something inside of it clicked together when she held it high and shook it—right at me. She drew closer and closer to me, shaking the bag and staring deep into my eyes.

It looked like a flash of light was passing through her eyes as she stared at me intently, then she tossed a muffled grunt my way, and carried on in her snakeskin belt and headband, swinging her snakeskin bag.

A long shiver ran down my spine, and my palms were suddenly sticky with sweat. I honestly didn't know if she *had been throwing good energy or bad energy my way. It was important to know in a world of juju—black magic and witches. The only thing I did know was that my market stroll was no longer fun. I leaned against the stinky meat stall for support, watching her back move through the crowd.*

CHAPTER 1

I SHOULD HAVE KNOWN THE DAY WHEN, OUT of the clear blue, my mom said, "Honey . . ." That "honey" was a dead giveaway that she was going to spring something big on me. She saves that word for major occasions. Like for bad news along the lines of "Honey, your father and I are going to get a divorce." Or for when I'm really sick. So this "honey" could only mean trouble, because I wasn't sick. And she was already divorced.

"Honey, what do you think about moving?" That day she smoothed her skirt like she didn't have a care in the world. Definitely too casual. The setting sun was beaming through our big kitchen window, highlighting a strange shine in her eyes.

"No thanks. We just got settled here in San Diego, and I've just made some friends. Good friends. Do you remember how long it took me to make friends in Palo Alto? Or San Luis Obispo? I'm not Ms. Friendly like you, so no, I don't want to move. Why should we move? Did you get fired?"

"No, I didn't get fired. Why didn't you ask if I got promoted?" She squatted down in front of me and took both my hands. "Jodie, a chance of a lifetime has come up, and we can't let it pass us by."

"Whose lifetime—yours or mine?" I took my hands out of hers. I know my mother too well. "And where would this great chance take us?"

The look in her eyes, sort of like pain crossed with fright, made it clear that this really wasn't a discussion. Her mind was made up. I could tell by the way she sucked her lower lip into her mouth, and doodled with her finger on the tabletop. "Well, actually I was thinking about Africa. Sierra Leone in West Africa."

"Why not the moon?" I asked. "It must be closer." The whole idea was so off the wall that I prayed she was joking. She continued to doodle, and I suddenly knew that she was dead serious.

"Uh, like how soon are we talking? Do I have time to tell my soon-to-be ex-best friends good-bye? Should I buy them Christmas presents, or do you expect to be gone before then? What about my life? Does it just get put on hold while we do your thing? Do I have any say at all?"

Relief and excitement swept across her face like a brush fire in the wind. "Sure, you have time to tell Lisa,

Gina and Felix good-bye." She began counting on her fingers like some little kid. "Let's see, five weeks? No sense Christmas shopping, but we'll have a big Thanksgiving dinner here with whoever you want to invite. Then before the wishbone has dried enough to break, we'll be outta here."

I looked at her closely. "Outta here, Mom? Isn't that pretty quick to be, as you say, 'outta here'?" My friends are always talking about what a cool, beautiful mom I have, but "outta here" in a month was something new. I looked at her light brown hair with its few streaks of gray, and her sky-blue eyes that catch looks from strangers all the time. Her slightly crooked smile made her look years younger than thirty-eight, but not young enough for talking like my friends and me.

When we were a family—before my dad decided he needed a new one—I loved to sit between my parents and listen to them talk about me. "Jodie Nichols, You've got the best of both of us," my dad would say. Tugging on my braid, he'd say, "My gorgeous blond hair," and then he'd flick my long eyelashes, "and your mom's killer blue eyes." He'd run his finger down my nose like a skier heading down a steep slope. "You are blessed with my distinguished nose," then circling my mouth, "And your mother's crooked smile."

"Don't forget my brains," Mom would always throw in, then we'd all laugh.

I shook the memory away and said, "Outta here?" again. "We aren't discussing it at all? Is this a done deal?"

"Oh, Jodie, honey, listen. I've gotten funding for my fieldwork from the university, with a year's sabbatical to go to Bukama, the fishing village where I want to work. It's taken more than a year to arrange, and today, Jodie, today they finally said yes."

I noticed her doodling fingers had started rapping the tabletop, and her eyes were filling with a light that was coming from somewhere deep inside. "It's my old Peace Corps village. Just think, Jodie, I had to wait until I was twenty-three to get there, but you get to go at fourteen."

That obviously struck her as better news than it did me. It kind of sounded like a good idea, and it kind of didn't. What would I do there? And how could I live without my friends? Ever since my folks' divorce we had bounced from central and northern California to the very south of the state. Every place we went my mom made friends in no time, but not me. I'm as shy with strangers as my mother is fearless. Sometimes I get sick of seeing how she can do anything she sets out to do.

"I can barely make friends in America, so how will I do it in Africa?" I asked her.

"Oh, honey, you'll make friends. First you'll learn the language and then before you know it you'll be making friends with everyone you want to."

"Learn the language?"

"Krio, dear. It's not too hard." She was holding my hands again, squeezing them with each word. "It's an English dialect, so you'll recognize some of the words right away. Actually, there are eighteen tribes in Sierra Leone, Jodie, and nineteen languages. Krio is the language tribes use between themselves and strangers.

"Oh, Jodie, don't close your mind to the idea. How many of your classmates will ever have the chance to go live in an African village?"

She played with my fingers while she said, "I promise you, if you're totally miserable we'll come home. Right back here to San Diego and your same school and same friends. But you have to promise me to try and make it work. It will be an adventure, I promise you. Say you'll go, and say you'll try to make it work."

I looked at her, scowling. "You've had a year to get used to the idea, and I've had five minutes. You think that's fair? Give me some time, that's all I ask. Just give me some time."

EARLY THE NEXT MORNING I STOOD IN front of the school with Felix, Lisa and Gina. Kids were zooming past us on their way to first period. I had just told them I was moving to Africa. Felix was staring at me, mouth hanging open, like a man frozen in time.

Gina flung her arms wide, sending her notebook into a passing kid's head, knocking his sunglasses to the ground. Lisa sent silent, darting looks at me as she watched the whirlpool of kids swarm around us.

"It's true. In five weeks—thirty-five days from today, to be exact—we're leaving." I hate to admit it, but I loved their reactions: Felix frozen, Gina wild and Lisa deep in contemplation. It was exactly their three characters, each caught in a moment of concentration that I'd never seen before.

"Are you out of your mind?" Gina finally said. "There are jungles and snakes and spears over there. Tell your mom that she can risk her life, but not yours. You can live with us."

"That's right," her mirror-image twin, Lisa, whispered as if talking to herself. "There are diseases in Africa. I once saw a TV show about leprosy in Africa. You could get it and come back with no nose. Or lose all your fingers. Maybe even your ears will fall off. Then you'd never get any dates when we go to college." That's Lisa, always planning ahead.

With these terrifying pictures running through my mind I suddenly heard Felix. Felix and I had been friends for more than a year. He was the brother I didn't have, and the first person to talk to me at my new high school.

He looks just like the "l" in his name, long and skinny. His triangular eyeglass frames let you know right away that he's not your usual kind of guy. I have never seen him, no matter how hot it is, go anywhere without his jean jacket. Written across the back in bright red script is *The Cat*. Felix without his jacket would be like the Pope without his hat—it just doesn't happen. His curly black hair looks very relaxed on his head, but his mind is always busy. When he started rubbing the top of his right ear, I knew that the wheels were turning.

I wasn't surprised when his first question was, "Can I go? I've always dreamed of going to Africa. Just think, lions and elephants and aardvarks, still free like they should be. And the moon! I read that a full moon in Africa is something you have to see to believe. Imagine, drums beating in the moonlight. Living a simple life, like Americans did one-hundred-fifty years ago."

Just then Gina cut in. "Yeah, imagine life with no MTV, no shopping malls, no Valentine's Day school dances. BOOOOOORING," she dragged out.

"I can't remember," Lisa said, obviously still off in a mental horror show, "if leprosy makes your hair fall out. Maybe it's just your toes and ears and lips that fall off."

Felix waved his hand at Lisa to stop her rattling on. "Just think, Jodie, you'll have African friends. What do kids do there for fun on Saturday nights? Or Sundays? What language will you speak, where will you go to school, do you know what they eat?"

"Probably crocodile burgers," Gina piped in.

Felix continued, taking no notice of her. "Where will you live? Will you have a house, or a hut, or a tent. . . . Wait, why are you going there?"

I could have hugged Felix for the questions. He took my mind off of Gina's fears and Lisa's fascination with missing limbs. "My mom is going to study women in a fishing village. See what their lives by the sea are all about. Typical anthropologist stuff. I'll do correspondence courses. And I'm sure I'll make friends sooner or later. I mean, kids are kids, aren't they? And they speak a sort of English, called Krio."

Looking me straight in the eye, he asked, as if our lives depended on it, "Are you sure you won't need a man around?"

I shrugged, because I didn't know *what* we were going to need around. "For all I know, we may need a shrink before this is over."

"Will you write?" he asked me.

Looking back, straight into his eyes, I said, "Sure. Providing my fingers don't fall off."

2

THE WEEKS FLEW PAST AND I FOUND MYSELF totally confused. I was suddenly Someone at school, with kids who always just nodded at me in the past going out of their way to yell to me things like, "I'm jealous!" or "Take me!" or "Africa—COOOOL!" It was my moment of fame and I loved it. Too bad I couldn't stay and enjoy it.

And then there was the part of me that was actually growing eager to go. So many kids thought it was cool, why shouldn't I? I played a mental Ping-Pong game, bouncing between stay or go? With a flash of clarity I don't usually have, the answer came to me. Aloud I said, "If I stay, then I'll no longer be special. And if I go, I'll always be special."

Then one afternoon, four days before we were to leave, Felix said to me, "Jodie, do you have any idea how lucky you are? You have the power of change right in your little old hands—the rare chance to be whoever you want to be in a whole new culture, with totally new people. Nobody will have any expectations of you. A whole new Jodie may pop out.

"And just think, gone are the same old faces in the same old building, day in, day out. No more swim practice, or reading for the blind after school. No more school as we know it! Adios malls, movies and Taco Bell. Hello FREEDOM!"

Once he put it this way, I had to agree. *But would I be brave enough to change?* I wondered. And then like a flash of lightning I thought, *What would I change?* But that just added to my confusion. First it was STAY or GO? Then it was SCARED or EXCITED?

Slowly, like molasses creeping uphill, I started to get excited. There was definitely no doubt how my mom felt. It was written all over her face—in fact, it was written all over her body. She almost glowed, all 5'7 and $^3/_8$ inches, 142 pounds of her. From the moment she told me, the crooked smile was a permanent fixture on her face, and it was contagious.

One evening we were eating a giant pizza with everything on it, in preparation for all the pizzas we wouldn't eat in the coming year, when she announced, "Jodie, you need to start practicing more Krio." She bit into her pizza, and a long string of cheese swooped down.

I took advantage of her cheese struggle to cut in and

to say, "There's time. Besides, I'm sure some people there speak some English." We had started practicing greetings, like "Ow di go de go?" But I felt stupid talking a language that sounded a lot like baby talk to me.

"You'll regret it if you try to get away with only speaking English. You'll miss half the experience, and be very lonely if you can't make some friends. It really is a fun language, yes, fun, if you'd just let yourself go." Dropping her mouth open, she said, "Repeat after me, ahhhhh, like at the doctor's office. That's how you say 'I'."

"Later, Mom, I'm not in the mood right now," I said. I took a huge bite of my pizza and burned the roof of my mouth. That was the end of the language lesson that day.

We spent a lot of time discussing our new life in the village. "There is no point in worrying about what you won't have there, because you'll have more new things than you can imagine," she told me our last Saturday morning at home as we packed the kitchen things away.

"Like leprosy?" I asked her.

She threw her head back and let loose a laugh I hadn't heard in years. "Have you been talking to Lisa again?" she asked.

As our departure date grew closer, I had noticed that my mom had changed. She looked younger. And prettier than she had for a long time. She'd cut her brown hair short, and seemed to walk with more bounce in her step.

Someone on the street might pass her and think, *There goes a lady in love.* But there was no new boyfriend as far as I knew. Just Africa.

"Things will be very different. The food will definitely be different, and the way people dress. The pace will be much slower, especially out in Bukama.

"You might even suffer from something we call culture shock when we first get there, Jodie. But don't worry, you'll get over it as things become more normal to you."

I noticed she said this without really looking at me.

"Culture shock? Is this one of the diseases Lisa saw on TV?" I asked. "I mean, will it hurt or anything?" I knew what it meant.

Another big laugh burst forward, and she leaned across the table and started tapping on the back of my hand. "Oh, Jodie, we're going to have a great time . . . the colors, the sights, the sounds, the smells. Everything will be so new and different that you may never want to come back."

My eyes shot wide open, and I started to ask exactly how long she intended to stay—like more than a year?— when there was a knock at the back door. Felix was standing there, in his jacket, a globe tucked under his arm. He had been hanging around my mom like a lovesick pony ever since he had heard about our trip. He'd offered to accompany us, but that didn't work.

Then he'd asked if we needed someone to carry our bags, but my mom told him no on that account too. Now he mainly had endless questions.

"Just in time," I told him. "We're discussing the first disease I'll get in Africa."

He turned to my mom with a worried look, and she said, "We were talking about culture shock. It's easy to feel overwhelmed by so many new sights and sounds."

"Don't forget the smells," I threw in.

"I know I'd have no problems." Felix turned his serious gaze on my mom. "I should go to help Jodie with it."

My mom grabbed him and hugged him, surprising both of us. "Maybe you should come with us after all," she said with a laugh. I knew she didn't mean it, so I changed the subject quickly. No sense getting his hopes up for nothing.

"What's with the globe, dude?" I asked as I took it from him. He was still staring at my mom, trying to see if there was any seriousness in her last remark. I asked him again, louder. He put his finger on San Diego, then slowly rolled the globe toward Africa. We watched with fascination as his finger trailed across the U.S. and the big Atlantic Ocean.

"Time zones," he said. "Will we all be in the same day, or are you moving into the future?" Leave it to Felix.

"Yes and no," my mom said as she packed her blender into a storage box. "We'll be eight or nine hours ahead.

When you are having breakfast, we'll be fixing dinner. Then when you're having lunch, we'll be sleeping. By dinner time, we'll be into tomorrow while you're still in today."

"I'll call you and let you know what weather to expect," I said.

"Will you have a phone?" Felix totally ignored me.

"Heavens no," said my mom, "we won't even have electricity."

She said it like someone bragging about something. I glanced at Felix, glad he was around to ask questions I hadn't thought of. It hadn't even occurred to me that such a possibility existed. I looked at my mom and asked, "What other secrets are you hiding?"

"I have no secrets. Ask and I'll tell," she said, like someone singing a toothpaste jingle.

"Is that why we're traveling so light?"

"That's part of it. You won't need your hair dryer, or your stereo, or your roller blades, or a vacuum cleaner, or any appliance for that matter."

Felix was getting a goofy look in his eyes, and started carrying on about the "simple life."

I could see me, my elbows in suds, cleaning up after a goat stew by candlelight. "So what do we need, besides my Walkman?"

"Well, obviously we need some clothes, but not a lot of those either. Mainly cotton stuff, because it does get hot. And we'll need your school materials. Different medicines, which reminds me, we get our shots tomorrow."

"Shots!" I screeched. "Nobody ever said anything about any shots before."

Felix cut right in. "Shots against yellow fever and meningitis and cholera and malaria and . . ."

"Most of those, yes. And a few more, like a rabies vaccine. But we won't need shots against malaria because we'll just take some pills once a week against that." Now my mom sounded like someone saying, "Oh yeah, and hold the mustard."

I ran over to the phone and started dialing.

"Who you calling?" Felix asked.

"Gina and Lisa. I want to know if their offer to live with them is still good." Both my mom and Felix laughed. Then, picking up our silverware lying on the table, he said, "Come on, let's finish this packing."

chapter

3

STEPPING FROM THE PLANE INTO SIERRA
Leone was like walking into a wet blanket. The heat
swallowed us. I was drenched with sweat before we hit
the runway. I looked at my mom and said, "Hey, if it's
this cool at eleven-thirty at night, think what twelve
noon will be like."

She wasn't listening though. She looked like a
woman in a trance. Like she couldn't take enough in at
one time. She breathed in deeply, sucking in a lungfull of
soggy air.

"Mom, are you still here?" I asked. She looked at my
face sweating drops as big as grapes, and said with a wide
smile, "It's great to be back."

Lungi International Airport was like none I'de seen
before. Up on the roof, announcing our location, was a
falling-apart sign. The L hung at half mast, and the word
"International" was missing all its Ts. A fire truck with

two flat tires sat tilted beneath the broken sign, and cows grazed, at midnight, along the side of the runway.

I stumbled in a little pothole on the tarmac as we walked to the terminal, because only one cockeyed, dim lamp lit the way. Two rectangles of light from inside fell onto the ground on either side of the narrow door people were crowding through. As I was pushed along in the rush, I noticed that there was no glass in the windows, and I turned just in time to see my mom walk through one of the empty window frames, followed by a flow of people.

Inside, the noise was incredible. The immigration officer didn't look nearly as happy as my mom about being there. He looked like he needed a bucket to wring out his uniform in. My mom said, "Ow di bodi?" He grunted in response.

In the baggage area chaos reigned. "Watch for the bags," my mom said, "and grab them as quickly as you can."

That seemed obvious to me, I mean, I have traveled before. This was our fourth move since the divorce, though I admit, it was definitely a bigger move than the rest, and I felt as if I'd left more than the North American continent. I felt like I was on another planet.

Total madness raged around us. People that looked like porters without uniforms lunged at the bags as they came through a square cut in the wall. Passengers lunged just as fast. The total confusion seemed like a cross between a fire alarm in a crowded disco and a serious session of roller derby. Mom amazed me as she waded into the madness, elbows flying, ready for action.

Our first bag appeared and she fought over the handle with a very fat man wearing torn shorts. Once again she switched into her new (or old) language, and shouted, "Lef mi bo!" Whatever it meant was effective. She slung the bag back in my direction and said, "Hang on to it, Jodie."

The second bag proved much more challenging. A big man, standing a foot taller than my mother, moved in to grab it. She dipped beneath his huge sweating arm and snagged the handle. His hand, slick with sweat, slipped off as she pushed her way through the crowd toward me. We passed through customs with ease, especially compared to the baggage area, and my mom immediately disappeared into the biggest hug I've ever seen.

I stood there like a bump on a log until my mom's smiling faced surfaced and she remembered me. Taking me by the hand, she said proudly, "Ma Kargbo, Ah wan fo yu to meet my daughter, Jodie. Jodie, meet my old friend, Ma Kargbo." Before I could extend my hand, the biggest woman I've ever seen wrapped me in this awesome hug. I couldn't believe it. She didn't even know me, and she was this happy to see me.

My head was smashed against two great huge breasts. She smelled of wood smoke and cheap perfume. Her gown, a deep royal blue, had beautiful gold embroidery across the front. Her head was covered in the same rich colors.

She held me back from her and said, "Ow di go de go?" I looked at my mom for help, and she laughed and said, "Tell her 'Fine-o'." I did as I was told, then looked on with wonder as Ma Kargbo picked up my suitcase and put it on her head. With perfect balance and not even a sign that the bag weighed thirty pounds, we walked toward the exit. "Wi dun reech," my mom said to no one in particular.

We fought our way out the door, where Ma Kargbo pointed to a dilapidated green car slowly moving toward us and said, "My son, Prince, he de come jus now."

Winding his way through man-pulled wooden carts, bicycles, and an assortment of crashed-up-looking cars and trucks, Prince's smile glowed through the windshield, his progress as slow as a turtle. All the vehicles were pointing whichever way they wanted, and it looked like a slow motion version of Demolition Derby. Two small boys jumped on the trunk of Prince's car for a ride through the confusion. It suddenly dawned on me that the guys who were porters inside fighting for bags were now taxi drivers outside fighting for passengers.

One guy, dressed in uneven khaki shorts, a Bob Marley T-shirt and one red and one blue flip-flop, headed our way. He threw his arm up like someone catching a fly ball and pointed down at Ma Kargbo, yelling, "Sistah, I get one fine fine taxi. Which side yu go?"

He stopped dead in his tracks as Ma Kargbo took a deep breath and seemed to grow in size before our eyes. She waved one finger, side to side, in front of his sweating face. Not a word was spoken, but the taxi man turned quickly on his heel and crashed into the other taxi men following him over to try their luck. As one, they all turned and scrambled away.

Ma Kargbo looked my way, and her "Don't mess with me" look bloomed into a lighthouse-bright smile. She rearranged her royal blue headtie and said, "Power de," happy with herself. I stared at this big, beautiful woman with rounded cheeks and black skin that glistened like fresh hot tar and realized I couldn't guess her age. Her eyes shone young, and her immaculate straight white teeth sparkled. Small lines around her lips added an old touch to her face, and her body, almost disguised by her gown, was probably a lot like the Pillsbury Doughboy's. *Maybe she's forty-one or fifty-three*, I thought, *I really can't tell.* Just then the green wreck arrived.

Smiling proudly through a closed window, Prince drove up in a car that sounded like a blender full of loose screws. He screeched to a halt in front of us, then jumped out of his wreck. He wore a beautiful embroidered purple-and-black shirt, and had a soft matching cap on his head. He shook my hand very solemnly, then our eyes met and he burst into a grin that I almost needed sunglasses for. He looked my age, but he was driving so I assumed he was at least sixteen.

Prince opened the back door for me. It only took three kicks to get it open, then it hung at an odd angle. After I climbed in over a giant, bumpy green fruit or vegetable sitting on the floor, he slammed the crooked door hard, then pulled a short rope from his pocket and tied the door to the frame, making sure it stayed closed. Three windows wouldn't open, and a major spring had erupted through the upholstery. We drove slowly past lines of people walking in the moonlight with bundles on their heads. Banana trees lined the roadside, flicking leaves in the breeze.

We drove for about five minutes, down to a ramp leading to a car ferry that would take us across a bay to Freetown, the capital. The ferry seemed to soak up the moonlight, letting loose a nighttime shadow around its outline. It was two levels, vehicles on the bottom and people on top. Prince parked the car where a man told him to, came around and untied my door, then said in a beautiful lilting voice, "Let wi go see upside."

We joined a group of whooping women with large bundles on their heads and sleeping babies tied to their backs on a crowded staircase. It seemed like every single person was talking or laughing or poking or pinching.

I was actually glad my mom had someone else to talk to. It gave me a chance to just look and listen, and enjoy the ride across the bay. It was one of those nights that Felix dreamed about. The moon was bigger than I had ever seen it—as full as it could go, sending down a bright golden light on the water.

The whistle blew to announce our departure, and a few last-minute pedestrians came scrambling on. We pulled away from the land, and right away, moonbeams danced in the wake. Down the way from me, one man started tapping a beat on the railing. Then there were ten men playing the same rhythm, and soon the singing started. The men sang in deep, low voices, and the women sang loud and high. The beat increased, and an old bent woman began dancing. Five smiling women put their head bundles down and joined her. The babies sleeping on their backs bounced with the rhythm of their mother's bouncing behinds.

Clad in bright-colored gowns and headties, they grabbed kids to dance with them. One song ended and another started right away. There were women dancing together and alone at the same time, with no one the least bit embarrassed or self-conscious.

Suddenly I noticed my mom watching me, with a

huge smile spread across her face. And it occurred to me that I had a smile as big as hers.

Here I was, surrounded by people making music with their hands and feet and voices. Here I was, surrounded by people just happy to be alive. The deck of the ferry quivered with the vibrations of its dancing passengers as we chugged across the bay. It was contagious. My mom put her arms around me and Ma Kargbo and said, "Well Jode, what do you think?"

I didn't want to appear too gaga, so I said, "Now I know why we don't need our stereo." The three of us swayed with the driving beat, our arms around each other, and I thought, *What's going on?* I never dance with my mom, especially in public. Then I thought of Felix. Squinching my eyes tightly closed, I said out loud, "You would love it!" My mom leaned toward me and said, "What did you say, kid?"

"I was thinking of Felix," I told her. "You should have brought him, Mom. He would definitely love it."

"And what about you?" she asked nervously.

"Wait small—it's too soon to tell." All the while my foot tapped madly to the beat.

4

THE DRIVE THROUGH FREETOWN TO MA Kargbo's took forever. It was as if we were driving through a party. The streets vibrated with competing stereo speakers blaring African music and reggae from small bars lining the sides of the narrow streets. Young men slouched against wooden railings on the porches of the tiny square buildings blasting music.

Prince seemed to know everyone and he'd stop for handshakes out his mother's window since his wouldn't open, every five or ten feet. Friends would splay giant hands across the windshield, which he would match from inside, high-fives through the glass, and answering shouts of "Wetin you get?" from faces staring in at my mom and me.

Two young women, walking hand in hand in matching yellow-and-black gowns and headties, stood in front of the car. Prince rolled to a stop right up against their thighs as they shouted to him, "Eh bo, ow di bodi?"

Prince called back through the cracked windshield, "Na move youselfs jus now. Wi go see back later."

They laughed and waved, strolling off with their clasped hands swinging between them. "If wi no go see yu later, yu de get plenty palaver," the nearest one said as they got out of the road.

Ma Kargbo reached over the seat and grabbed my mother's knee. With her other hand she pointed at a tall mud wall up the road on the right. "Watch jus now," she said as the car turned toward a gate set back in the wall. The headlights beamed dimly on the blue gates, painted with five intricate hairdos and a sign in crooked, flaming-orange letters that said MA KARGBO'S FINE-O HAIR SA-LOON. WELL COME.

My mom shrieked like someone getting goosed, then leaned forward and hugged her old friend's shoulders. "It be beautiful pas words," she gushed. "Ow di busyness?"

"Sometimes slow like de turtle, na sometimes fas like de chicken runnin from de dog. Ah no get complaint," she said. As we drove through the gates, she grabbed a knee on each of us, "Na yu two be well come in yu own own home."

Our home for two days, I thought as I stared out the window at the collection of small mud buildings. Maybe Bukama would be better.

We parked at the end of a flat, dirt compound. Little

square huts, some covered in a white chalky paint and others the same color as the dirt, formed a border on three sides of the square. Two very tall palms guarded the gate, and a little patch of corn grew in a corner nearby. A blackened old teapot hissed away on three rocks set around a small fire.

My mom followed my gaze and said, "That's the kitchen." It was a tin roof supported by four twisted tree branches, connected by three straighter crossbars. A collection of clay and metal pots sat neatly stacked by one branch, and three smooth, golden-brown scoops hung from stubs sticking off a crossbar. *So that's a kitchen*, I thought, *a far cry from our white walls, blue shiny counters, and built-in appliances back home.*

With a wide sweep of her arm Ma Kargbo announced, "Wi get storerooms, sleep rooms, eat room and rainy-day hair room." Her sweeping arm stopped on a round little building standing alone in the compound's center. Its mud walls reached halfway up the support poles, and was covered by a neat thatched roof. Hammocks swung from pole to pole. "Dat be de bafa. De talk room."

Then my mom pointed to a small shedlike building across the compound that was obviously isolated from everything else. "That," she said with drama, "is a place you need to know. It's the latrine, also known as the toilet in America. Come on, I'll show you."

I hung back and said, "You think I forgot how to use a toilet?" This whole place was getting too strange.

"Not at all, dear, but this is probably different from any toilet you've ever used before. Just come with me, I'll give you a few tips, and then you're on your own." She took off, as if she was in desperate need of it herself, and I slowly followed.

It was a slightly leaning mud structure with a door made from scrap wood that didn't quite reach the top, and no windows. My mom took a flashlight from her pocket and said, "First, I always check for snakes before entering." She flashed her light into the square of darkness inside, looking first around the floor, then along the sticks that served as rafters.

"Then I check for spiders. Not all spiders are dangerous, but I always feel better if I'm in these places all alone."

This time the light moved more slowly and I got a good look around. My heart hit my belly as I took it all in. It had a dirt floor, and a well-worn plank set a few inches above the floor on a ledge made of dirt. In the center sat a round piece of wood with a handle attached to it. My mom lifted the wooden circle by its handle and showed me a carved hole that looked like a circle of darkness. "The poop shoot," she laughed.

Then, flashing her light on either side of the hole, "See these footprints here?" She stepped with precision on two spots worn smooth and deep on each side of the little wooden lid. Standing tall in the stinky, scary black box, she announced, "Now I'll share with you my own personal technique."

Bending over, she set her flashlight down, pointing up at the roof. "Step One: I place my torch beside me, light facing up, so I don't have to be here in total darkness."

Then, squatting like she did to weed the garden in San Diego, she said, "Step Two: I get as comfortable as possible, but also ready to make a quick getaway if necessary."

Lifting the lid with her right hand, she slid it to the side. "I do this last so I don't have to smell anything for too long."

I stood transfixed, watching my mom squatting, the light of the torch sending an eerie upward glow on her face. "Unfortunately, even though I am in place, I don't need to use it right now. When I'm done though, I take a piece of paper off this pile, do my thing like I do back home, slide the lid back in place, stand up, then I'm out of here as fast as possible.

"It's crucial, Jodie, that the lid is back in place, otherwise flies get into the hole and carry out little pieces of . . ."

"I get it," I said, like someone on a game show pressing their buzzer.

"Would you like to try?" she asked me.

The thought of climbing into a dark, mud box with a crooked wooden door made me feel faint. The realization that this was now my life made me feel sick. My mom's eyes and Ma Kargbo's smiling face were watching me, waiting for an answer.

With a shrug I said, "Now or never. Might as well, then I don't have to come back later."

I went through the whole process—first running my tunnel of light from my torch slowly around the roof and beams, like a dentist doing a thorough molar check-up, only looking for snakes. I couldn't believe I had to do a snake check to go to the bathroom. I was relieved to see that the roof and walls didn't meet, for that meant some fresh air would get in there when the door was closed.

Trying to look cool and calm as my heart beat like a stopwatch, I did the spider check, then prepared for the dreaded moment of stepping inside. With determination I put a foot on each groove. Taking a loud, deep breath, I bent to place the flashlight upright, then dropped into a deep squat. I'd thought I'd done all the steps necessary to complete what had once been an easy, natural process, when my mom laughed.

"Hey Jodie," she said, "just like at home, it works better if you take your pants off first."

I stood straight, stared at my mom until she shut the

door, then dropped my pants and took care of business as fast as I could. I reached for a paper and found that it was a selection of old magazines, newspapers and a torn-up book about English grammar. At first I thought it was for reading while you did your thing, but then I thought, *Who in their right mind would stay in this dark little shack to read?* Grabbing a piece, I wiped myself with a quick swipe, then bolted from the smelly blackness.

Ma Kargbo was waiting with my mom when I burst free into the fresh air and moonlight. Grabbing my shoulders in her big and powerful hands, she steered me toward a sleep room. Inside the dark, hot box-of-a-room were two narrow beds with lumpy, hard-looking mattresses. A lone candle, standing in a pool of hot melted wax on one of the two windowsills, shed the slightest of light on the room. She patted my shoulders with little bouncing slaps, then reached around me and hugged me from behind. "Wi go see tamara," she said as she pushed me down on the bed. Turning at the doorway she said, "Na sleep de peaceful sleep."

5

I WOKE THE NEXT MORNING IN A POOL OF sweat. I'm not sure I really even slept. One rooster started crowing long before daylight, which woke up every other rooster in town, as well as me. Obviously no one had told them that they are supposed to start at sunrise. As the morning light started to filter slowly into the hut, I could see the wall beside me was covered in photographs cut from magazines.

Every kind of photo you can imagine—car ads, the smoking cowboy, snow peaks and Los Angeles skyscrapers, sailboats and Tina Turner were stuck to the smooth mud walls. Calendars—from 1974 through 1997—filled in the other spaces. Like a baby, my mom slept peacefully beneath a velvety picture of dogs playing pool. I could hear a rhythmic thumping sound from outside, and thought, *These folks sure like to dance.*

The fierce sunlight nearly blinded me as I stepped out of the dark hut. Six little kids, some dressed in ragged shorts or long T-shirts, and one wearing only a string of leather pouches around her neck, swirled around me, shrieking. I thought they were playing tag when one tiny little guy got pushed into my leg and he ran off wailing as if he'd just touched fire. It was definitely a game of dare—how close can you get to the strange new white girl without getting touched? Sheer panic was the loser's prize.

The thumping sound came from two women, alternately pounding long wooden sticks into a tall wooden container. One woman pulled her stick out as the other dropped hers in. Just like the oil pumps along the coast back home. I jumped when Prince suddenly said behind me, "De be making da breakfast."

As we watched, my mom finally wandered out, wrapped in a colorful cloth like the local women. I did a double take, realizing that she looked good. Also, the lapa looked much cooler than the jeans sticking to my skin. She sauntered over, walking casually through the quacking ducks and playing kids.

"Sleep well, dear?" She looked as if she'd had a peaceful night, which almost made me angry.

"Great," I said, "if you don't mind waking up more tired than when you went to bed." She was going to respond when Ma Kargbo came blowing out the door. She moved with a grace that her size should have discouraged. Swooping down with one arm, she grabbed a baby from what must have been a five-year-old girl. Then she nudged a goat with her knee, sending it bleating across the yard.

She grabbed me into a hug with her and the baby, and said, "Ow di bodi?"

"She's asking 'How are you?' " my mom said. "Tell her, 'Ah be fine-o.' "

I could barely breathe, smothered in her major chest. The kid in her arms was pulling my hair gently and slapping me on the head. I looked at my mom pleadingly with my right eye.

"You know, Jode, you have to start sometime. Or else you'll have a pretty boring year. Not talking to anyone. Not making any friends. Just say, 'Ah be fine-o. Ow di go de go?' It means, 'I'm fine. How is it with you?' You know, like we did in our kitchen back home. Try it, Jodie. Try it for me. Before you know it you'll be talking like a local."

"That's good, huh? Talking like a local?" I could hear the working women with my exposed right ear talking behind me, and realized I understood nothing they were saying. This language thing was just like the outhouse—in my face. No time to adjust or ease into things.

"You said this was like English, you sure could fool me," I said with a scowl. The chances of me understanding, much less speaking it, seemed as good as an M&M staying solid in the sun. And I wasn't feeling too keen about my adventurous mother either, getting me into this mess, when suddenly it occurred to me that we were having this conversation while I was buried in the world's biggest, wettest hug.

My mom just got her wise-guy smile when she saw I realized this. "What will it be?" she asked. "And for your information, the language those women are speaking"—she pointed at the women with the sticks—"is Mende, not Krio. So you don't have to worry if you don't understand anything. I don't either."

Ma Kargbo, still waiting for my answer to her greeting, squeezed me tighter to her and the baby. I'm not really into hugging. Plus, it must have been five hundred degrees. I thought, *One more squeeze and I'll squirt out the bottom of her arms like a broken tube of toothpaste.* Her hugs seemed to say, "Go ahead, just try."

Without looking at my mother I said, "Ah be fine."

Ma Kargbo stepped back to look at me and said, "Yu de talk na fine-o."

She gave me a smile that made her face shine like those buttons hippies used to wear. And I had to smile back. She pulled a cloth from the folds of her gown and wiped my sweating face and arms. "You'll be speaking Krio in no time," she said to me in perfect English.

My eyes popped open wide, and my mom laughed. "Surprise! Ma Kargbo's English is great, but you won't learn Krio speaking English. So just relax, Jodie, and don't worry, dear, you'll get over your culture shock soon."

My mom was a woman with a mission. After breakfast she said, "Today we shop, and tomorrow we go to Bukama. And so, my dear, are you ready to go shopping jus now?"

I said yes, but once we left the compound I knew I wasn't. I thought life inside the compound was strange, but outside the blue gates was a zillion times worse. Chaos had replaced the activity of the night. A noisy, busy, crowded chaos filled the streets. Women dressed like rainbows walked smoothly beneath giant trays filled with pineapples, papayas and bananas perched squarely on their heads. Growing out each side of one woman's waist were two tiny feet, attached to a small baby wrapped snugly on her back in a cloth sling tied around her chest and lower belly. I wanted to grab those sweet little feet, but controlled myself. The pink little feet bottoms stuck out like air-conditioning units, the only thing revealed besides the head. A closer look showed almost every woman, and lots of girls my age or younger, carried babies on their backs.

We walked along a dusty road with the throngs, past cars stuck at a standstill in the road. People swarmed around them like they were just so many boulders strewn in the way. Four old men in white skull caps and faded tie-dye shirts, passed a short burning stick around to light their clay pipes, then the last guy flicked it into the road. A young man in mirrored sunglasses and a green, yellow and black ski cap swooped down and collected the smoldering stick to light his cigarette. He passed it off to a woman fanning a small pot of coals in front of her tea stall. The sight of the coals brought a new layer of sweat to my saturated face and sticky jeans.

Rambling wooden buildings of chipped blue-and-green, yellow-and-purple paint lined the roadsides. An old man, dressed in a faded army uniform, chased chickens from inside his shop, and kids played Jump Over the Open Sewer. My mom stopped at a stall selling matches, kerosene and dried fish.

Trapped between an open sewer and a display of hanging, smelly dried fish, I couldn't resist asking with a gag, "Are these some of the great new smells you were talking about?"

"I never said good smells," my mom said, as a man, stooped under a pile of tires balanced on his shoulders, crashed into her. The tires bounced to the ground and took off in different directions. The first rolling disaster hit the back legs of a donkey pulling a cart loaded with long sticks. His back legs buckled briefly, but with a swift lash of his owner's stick, he regained his balance. Another tire left treads across my mother's foot, and a third crashed into the dented door of a taxi stalled next to us. The fourth did the most damage as it knocked over a stand selling hairpins, fake braids, combs, bras and soap. The woman glared at the tire man, who pointed at my mom, and said with a shrug, "Ow fo do? She be de problem." Slowly he collected his tires, and two men loaded them on his shoulders as he bent in half, then took off running.

We hadn't been out on the street for twenty minutes yet, but the noise, the heat, the stench! I found myself clutching the side of a crooked stall when Prince suddenly appeared. He shook my hand as if he were pumping water, and asked me, "Yu want fo drink someting cold?"

"YES!" I said, then blurted out, "I want to go home."

"Which side home? America home or here home?" he asked, clearly worried.

I wanted to blurt out America, but his face seemed to plead with me to like his place. So I said, "Dis home."

His perfect smile filled his face, and like some fancy restaurant guy, he bowed me toward a man sitting next to a box filled with chunks of ice. Lifting a piece as big as a birthday cake, Prince called out, "Coca-Cola, Fanta, Sprite or palm wine?"

"Coke," I said, and he lifted a dripping bottle from the box and shocked me as he opened it with his teeth. I took it from him and lifted it to my parched lips. The cold slid down my throat and brought tears to my eyes. I fished a smaller piece of ice from the box and rubbed it across my forehead and cheeks. "Sorry, but I have never, ever been this hot before," I told the surprised Prince.

He paid the man, then walked me toward the compound. Moving through the crowd like an ambulance with lights flashing, he held my arm and shouted to people ahead, "Na move move, jus now. One weak weak woman she de pass." The masses parted like the Red Sea, and we reached the compound in no time.

I FELL BACK AGAINST THE GATE AS WE SHUT out the noise and madness, taking several deep, wet breaths. Turning to Prince, I said, "Now I know how you got your name."

His smile said he understood what I meant, and he whistled as he started back out the gate, shoulders swaying in beat to his own personal song. I grabbed the gate before it shut, "Please, tell my mom Ah de wait here." That was if he found her and if she even noticed I wasn't there.

I spent the morning watching Ma Kargbo braid the hair of a young girl called Flora. First she took a porcupine quill and divided Flora's hair down the middle, then she divided the right side in half down the side of the head. Each half was divided in half again, and using her quill like a painter uses a brush, she drew a rigid line down the side of Flora's scalp, separating the finest lines of hair aside.

I tried to follow her hands, but they moved too fast for the human eye as she plaited a neat, tight row of hair into a perfect braid that hugged Flora's scalp. Once she got started, the rows seemed to grow like crops in a field. Ma Kargbo kept up a steady stream of conversation and laughter as she worked, as if her hands belonged to someone else. I wasn't listening though. The first half of Flora's head was done in about an hour, and as Ma Kargbo put the finishing touches to the second half, I kept thinking about what my mom had gotten us into. Peeing had become a production. I hadn't slept because of roosters and sweat. The streets were like mini riot scenes. Maybe I could just live in this compound for a year, learning to braid hair while ignoring the crazy world outside. I was tired, hot and unhappy when finally my mother dragged in through the gates.

She was laden with bags and trailing a stream of kids carrying parcels wrapped in newspaper for her. Her face was flushed, and a smudge of black showed on her foot where the tire had passed. She raised a kerosene lantern in one hand and a net bag filled with batteries, cans of tomato paste, a hammer, new flip-flops and a few of those cloths called lapas, and shouted, "We're ready, bright and early tomorrow morning. We're outta here!"

6

"PLOP DOWN ANYWHERE YOU SEE A SEAT," my mom told me as we joined the shoving masses entering the bus. The bus was really a big truck with wooden benches separated by an aisle down the middle. A tilted tin roof offered shade from the sun that was scorching the earth and my brains. The worn wooden benches shined like rocks polished smooth by raging water. A sign over the door read PASSENGERS: 33 + 1. I think they were all on my seat.

I sat on a bench for two, with two women, four kids and two roosters, one cheek hanging over the aisle. On the floor next to me was a young woman sitting on bags of cassava, a root vegetable they eat. She had her head on my knee and was fast asleep. A guy behind me had his knee in my side. There was an armpit in my nose and an elbow in my cheek. A bag of chickens sat on my right foot and a man stood on my left.

Horror filled me as I thought about our conversation

the night before. Would I really have this girl's head on my knee for nine hours? And an armpit stuck in my nose for 220 miles? I'd asked my mom, "How can two-hundred-twenty miles take nine hours? That's like driving thirteen miles per hour? Nobody goes that slow."

I'll never forget how she smoothed her lapa with two long strokes down her thighs. "Well dear, when you see the roads, you'll understand. But it'll be fun, seeing new sights and meeting new people."

I shrugged away the memory, and stared out the space that is usually a window, trying not to think about the trip ahead. Young guys my mom called bobos were handing up bulging, brown burlap bags to another squad of bobos on the roof. Each time a bag was caught it rained a few peanuts on their straining neck and shoulder muscles that shone like black wet marble. It was a nice view. Sparkling tin washbasins followed the peanuts, long stalks of sugarcane roped together followed the basins, along with jerry cans of bright-red oil and three rolled mattresses. After adding six bolts of green and orange-swirled cloth, the bobos climbed onto the roof to ride along with the goods.

I focused on the inside of the truck when the bobos disappeared. I was amazed. Bundles in soft bags were still coming in through the windows. I was sure there was never any room, but everything was pushed and wedged and shoved patiently, and each bundle fit somewhere. A little kid with no pants was the final bundle passed in.

The young woman near the window hauled him into the bus, then placed a whopper kiss on his cheek. Smiling, she passed him over one passenger to an old woman. The old woman next to me also gave him a loud kiss and then passed him to me. I didn't know if we were kissing and passing him for good luck or what, and I might not love where I was, but I wasn't going to let everyone know, so I took him and planted a big kiss on his cheek.

His eyes bulged in his round, little black face, the whites of his eyes shone like street lamps in a dark, moonless sky. Just as the first yowl of fright escaped him, the man in the aisle reached down and took him from me. No kiss, so I guess it wasn't part of a travel charm.

The smell in the bus was outrageous. The combination of goats and chickens doing their things right on the floor of the truck, and people sweating like machines made a killer stink. It singed my nose hairs, and burned the roof of my mouth if I tried breathing with my mouth open. A bag of dried fish had its own rank smell to add to the stink. I kept trying to catch my mother's eye, but she was too busy being Ms. Friendly and didn't see me.

I tried quick, shallow breaths, but that didn't work on reducing the smell intake. Then I tried to take a deep breath, thinking I could hold it for long periods, but that didn't work either. The old woman next to me looked at me like a dog checking out a chicken.

Rivers of sweat flowed down my cheeks, and my blond hair looked dark brown, it was so drenched in sweat. My T-shirt looked like someone had thrown a bucket of water on me. It clung like Saran Wrap and I felt very embarrassed. It's not like I've got the world's biggest boobs, but I felt as if I was trying to show the world what I have. My jeans were already stained with little polka dots of sweat dripping off my chin. I seriously regretted not taking my mom's advice that morning.

She had handed me a lapa and said, "This will be much more comfortable, dear. Those jeans are gonna get hot and sweaty."

"No thanks," I said. "My jeans are the only normal things around me. They don't go."

She just shrugged and said, "Your choice."

Oh, how I regretted that choice, which isn't anything new. I tend to be a slow learner, with a real dislike for advice. I prefer to do things my way. It usually works out that the advice was right, and this was no exception. But I needed my jeans. I needed something "normal" in my life. And so I sat and sweated like a pig. I smiled weakly at the woman who was looking at me now as if a UFO had just landed next to her.

Shrugging her shoulders, she said, "Ow fo do?" She pointed to her own sweating face and soggy clothes, then lifted her palms and shrugged again. Somehow I knew she was saying, "What can you do?" I smiled and shrugged back.

With a last shout out the window of "Bukama, Bukama, Bukama," the driver ground his gears and we slowly pulled away. Just as the bus got underway and a little breeze began to stir—thank God—it stopped again to pick up another dozen people and animals. I couldn't believe it. The roof must have been full too, for people just hung off the back of the truck in layers.

It figured, the first passenger that wanted off was sitting in the farthest, darkest corner. Everyone in front had to get off, dragging bulky bags and containers of palm wine, amazingly good-natured about the major inconvenience. Each time someone got off, the others scrambled back on in hopes of improving their places. I clung to the bottom edge of the seat, hoping not to get swept off.

The day wore on as we careened down the bright red dirt roads, past villages of small huts with men hanging out in hammocks and women walking with huge bundles on their heads. Each time the poda-poda stopped I whispered to myself, "Please get off," while looking at the woman next to me, but she never did. She just kept leaning against me like a wet sponge. As the hours dragged on, my butt ached and my arm was completely stuck to hers. I moved my butt slightly to ease the bone in my right cheek, a bone that I'd never known about before. The girl sleeping against my leg awoke. She smiled shyly at me.

I wanted to be friendly, but my mood was worsening by the minute. I tried to smile back, but my muscles were clenched tight in a frown and refused to smile. My look must have been scary because she turned her head away with a snap of her neck, banging her chin on my knee.

"I'm gonna kill my mom," I whispered into the damp air under the sounds of a crowing rooster somewhere in the back and the clanging of metal parts. Twisting my head, I got a glimpse of her. She had a baby on her knee now, and the woman standing next to her in the aisle had her arm slung around my mom's shoulders like an old friend. They talked and laughed until my mom glanced my way and saw my face.

It was only for a split second, while the bodies between us all leaned into a curve of the wobbling truck. People hanging out the door screamed, which must have fit right in with the look on my face. Distress swept across my mother's face as our eyes met. She had just enough time to read my look of GET ME OUTTA HERE when the crowd between us stood or sat straight again, and my view of her was closed off by a wall of sweating bodies.

It was as if we were on different trips, and my mom was a different person. While I could hardly wait to get off, she looked completely relaxed, even though she was on the same hot, stinky vehicle as I was.

Suddenly the bus screeched to another halt. The passengers in the aisle all leaned forward with the momentum of the gasping brakes, and when bodies began to shift, I saw my mom move forward a few seats.

The man standing next to me leaned down to collect his bulging burlap bag, and my mom shouted to me, "Hang in there, kid." Slowly people wiggled their bodies and bundles down the crowded aisle, and I saw my mom leapfrog into the seat across from me. She was quick, landing in the seat before the woman moving had reached her full height. The baby tied to the woman's back in a lapa kept right on sleeping.

My mom tried to grab my hand, but it slipped out of her wet one. She cracked a smile. "Jodie, you okay?" I didn't answer her. She leaned across the aisle against the man's legs standing between us. "Remember, Jodie, No Condition Is Permanent."

I glared at her. "What's that mean?"

"It's the name of our poda-poda," she said. "It means that even this bus ride will end sometime." She pointed to the sign by the driver's head. "Every poda-poda has a name, like the one I saw this morning that's called To Be

A Man Is Not Easy. They write it across the front and back of the truck. Ours just happened to have the right name for this trip."

"Is that supposed to be funny?" I asked with my permanent new frown.

"Come on, Jodie, please give the place a chance. I know this is uncomfortable, but just hang in there for another hour or two."

"Hour or two?" I almost screeched. "And I don't call this uncomfortable. I call it torture. Another hour or two?"

"If we're lucky," she said with a definite cringe. "Jodie, this isn't Kansas. We could always break down, or get a flat and have no spare or run out of gas or hit a cow in the road. Just look at it all as part of the adventure."

"STOP!" I shouted. It came out so loud that all the people around us turned their heads toward me, like people watching a tennis match.

Even the driver heard my outburst, for he stood on his brakes and the truck careened to a stop. My mom's face flushed red under her coating of sweat. The man standing between us, a goat clutched to his chest like a sleeping baby, asked her something. She looked at me and said, "He wants to know if you have a bad belly and need to stop. What should I tell them?"

I felt myself blush like my mom, and thought we must look like a couple of cherries in a box full of raisins.

The whole thing was impossible, and only getting worse. I suddenly felt older than dirt, and did not want to fight. Even Felix wouldn't see this as a great thrill, and Lisa, she'd shake with the thought of catching some rare disease in the crowd. I didn't even want to think about what Gina would say. One thing was certain, my mom's idea of a good time and mine were two different things.

"Tell them I changed my mind." I turned my head away from her and stared out the window.

As I turned away I heard her say, "That's not the end of this conversation, young lady."

I ignored her, choosing to gaze out the far window. Two more hours kept echoing through my brain as the truck zoomed along in the gathering African darkness.

THERE WAS SOME RELIEF WITH THE SETTING sun, but a smell that could wither plants hung on, and I knew that I was in the worst mood of my life.

I was hot and sweaty and hungry and tired and pissed off by the time we finally got to the village. Even my mom looked bedraggled and soggy. The lines around her eyes that mean she's mad were etched deep like little canyons. We didn't speak as we gathered our suitcases. I was actually glad for the crowd of pushing kids that formed around us.

Cries of "poo-mui, poo-mui" filled the air as the kids

pushed and shoved each other at us. One little guy crashed into my side and went off screaming like a wounded cat, just like the kid at Ma Kargbo's. It was clear that he was scared to death by the contact.

Trying to make a little peace, I asked my mom, "Is Poo-mui where the poda-poda goes next?"

She surprised me by laughing out loud. That laugh of hers that I never heard before Africa became part of our life. Her mad lines smoothed out and she put her soggy arm around my soaked shoulders and turned me toward her. "Oh, Jodie, I know there's a lot to get used to, but please don't set your heart against this experience. Poo-mui is Mende, the first language of the people around here. It means, 'white person.' I only laughed because I just remembered how I made that same mistake when I got here sixteen years ago."

I took one long look around me. We were in an open space at the base of a tree as big as a California redwood. The ground was swept clean, and I could see a collection of round and square squat huts behind the jostling crowd of kids. Each hut sat alone, but shared a big common area. A radio blasted from somewhere, but with the huts stuck so close together it was difficult to know just where it was coming from. Was this our new home? These crowded-together little huts? A chorus of "poo-mui, poo-mui" filled the darkening sky, and I wondered what we had gotten into.

Just as I was about to collapse, an old man with skin black as carbon paper and hair white as fresh snow stepped forward and said, "Cusheo. Wetin wi go du fo una?"

My mom's eyes lit up and she said, "He wants to know what he can do for us."

"How about scatter the crowd for starters?" I said. I was nervous, but my mom looked giddy. Her whole face smiled, wiping the angry lines away like an eraser on a chalkboard.

She rocked me back and forth like she did when I was little. "We're going to make it, kid."

How did she know that? I looked around at the strange people, the strange little huts, heard all the unknown words bouncing off my brain like balls in a pinball machine, and wanted to cry. We traveled halfway around the world for this? I felt like climbing onto the same old crappy poda-poda and heading back to America, with or without my mom. She was as good as gone anyway—even now excitement filled her voice as she answered the old man. And I realized just how alone I felt.

The old man's face lit up like a torch when my mom said, "Cusheo, pa. Ah be Valerie Nichols. Yu no fo forget me?" He spread his arms wide and said, "Well come home. It be too too long since yu de leave us."

Suddenly from the crowd, a young girl came forward,

about my age. She had a lapa wrapped around her waist, and held something out to each of us. I didn't see the coconuts right away because I was staring. She was topless. My mom nudged me and said, "Quit staring. Take the coconut, and say, 'Una tank ya.' "

As the first drops of fresh coconut milk slid down my throat, I realized it tasted better than any soda I've ever had. I drank it till there was none left, tilting my head back as far as it would go. When I took the coconut away from my face, I snuck a look around and confirmed something shocking. My mom and I were the only women with tops on. All I could think of was my mom, back in our kitchen in San Diego, saying, "We're going to blend in as well as possible. Do everything like the locals. You'll love it."

She must have read my mind again, for she looked me in the eye and said, "Not everything, dear."

The coconut girl, totally unembarrassed about being topless, stuck out her hand and said, "Well come. Wetin yu nem?" She covered her heart with her right hand and said, "Ah bi Khadi." Her smile was shy and wide, and it struck me how beautiful she was.

"Ah bi Jodie," I told her. My mom's eyes snapped open wide when she heard I had answered the girl in Krio.

KHADI AND I HIT IT OFF RIGHT FROM THE
beginning. By the time I quit staring at her bare boobs
and looked in her deep brown eyes, I could see her staring at me with just as much intensity. We smiled at each
other, and something inside clicked. I knew, I just knew,
somewhere deep inside, that here was a friend and that
we were going to be tight.

That night, lying on a bed that must have a day job
as an ironing board, I told my mom, "I want to speak
Krio."

She was lying in a hammock. "You did great tonight,
Jodie. I was so proud of you. You sounded so good, people thought you could really speak Krio. Hanging out
with Khadi will be the best way to learn."

The hut was as hot as the inside of a car parked in the
sun all day. The air was so still that the candle flame
near my head stood rigid, as if it were made of wax too.
Spiderwebs dangled from the sticks holding up the tin

roof, and the two small windows on either side of the hut each had four bars set into them, and no curtains or shutters.

I looked under my bed for rats or anything else that might wander in, and saw a lone shiny black shoe sitting against the back wall. The table between my bed and my mom's hammock had a maze of deep knife cuts into it. A little net draped over the doorway hung limply in the still air. The hut's owner, Pa Sorie's wife, Ma Luba, settled on a straw mattress in the corner with two kids and a goat. Little snuffles came from my mom's hammock almost as soon as she said good night. By the time I finally fell asleep, in a room smaller than my bedroom at home, with five people and a goat, I was drifting in a pool of sweat.

I awoke much too soon, to the predawn crows of the village roosters. My mom was still snoozing in her hammock, her hair sticking up at odd angles like a punk rocker, her hand tucked under her chin like a baby. Ma Luba was just heading out the door of the hut, a baby tied to her back and a brightly painted headpan balanced on her head. The sunlight was slowly creeping through the door. Another sweaty scorcher began, but for the first time I didn't mind.

My mom didn't look like someone going anywhere in a hurry, so I quickly pulled on my soggy jeans, smoothed down my wrinkled T-shirt, and headed outside. The flowering flame trees were the first things I noticed as I left the hut. Seeing them the night before had not prepared me for their morning brilliance. Each bright-orange flower looked as if it were in a good mood.

I stretched with a groan. An amazing amount of activity was going on in the smoky dawn light. Only women, girls my age, and young kids were out and about. I was looking for one smiling face in particular, but didn't see it. I saw women bent over cooking fires with straight backs and legs preparing the morning meal together, and children around their legs like pecking chickens. Then I saw a girl my age with a large bucket on her head. Khadi! She waved as she floated toward me with her back straight and her bucket balanced perfectly.

"Ow di bodi?" I asked like some long-time Krio speaker. She smiled a smile that dimmed the morning light, and I wanted to kick myself for not trying to learn more, like my mom had tried to convince me back home. After hot-dogging with the greetings Prince had taught me, I had to fall back into English, and asked her where I could get some water to wash. "At the well, le wi two go," she said with a smile and shyly took my hand. Together we crossed the village I had only seen in the weak twilight the evening before.

By the early morning light I could really see for the first time how beautiful the village was. Most of the huts were exactly the same, round with pointed roofs covered with palm fronds. Like an old photo from *National Ge-ographic.* The walls were all made of mud, and some were covered with a peeling layer of white paint. Young girls swept the area in front of each hut, leaving the cleanest dirt I'd ever seen. The leaves of the palm trees around the huts scratched against each other in a very slight breeze. And then I heard it.

Off in the not-so-far distance was the thump of heavy surf—the ocean. I had known the village was on the shore, but I had forgotten until I heard the crash of big waves. Khadi caught my eye, so we walked out to the beach. I blurted out, "People pay big money to vacation on beaches that look like this."

The pure-white sand stretched for as far as my eyes could see. Small dug-out canoes parked on the beach looked like a line of taxis waiting for customers. Fishing nets draped from poles resembled fancy displays in shop windows. A few men gathered down the beach, watching the water as they talked.

Giant, froth-spewing waves rolled in, crashing on the shore. We called those waves "sand blasters" in San Diego, and I wondered if the sea ever calmed down enough to get in it. I felt Khadi watching me, probably waiting for me to explain my outburst or at least say it more slowly. Somehow I didn't want to say it again. The blue-green water, long white beach, and sense of calm watching the talking men gave me my first hint of the good things my mom remembered about Sierra Leone. Looking at Khadi I said, "I need to wash." Once again she took my hand and turned us toward the village.

I assumed that wherever we were going for water I could shower right away, but I was wrong. A group of about ten laughing girls, each waiting her turn with a container, stood at the main well. *Friends of Khadi?* I wondered.

The laughing and joking stopped as quickly and completely as someone hitting a pause button on a stereo when we walked up. The girls, dressed in bright lapas wrapped around their waists, still didn't have any tops on. Resting beside each girl was a water container, some shiny aluminum buckets and other used plastic oil containers or dim and dented tin cans. Suddenly I felt like my bra was showing or something. Every eye but Khadi's was on me. They all stared, then one girl said, as if she were testing me, "Cusheo. Ow di go de go?"

"Na fine-o," I answered. Everyone smiled, then the chatter and the laughter picked up again. I had passed.

Two girls pulling water up in big black containers glistened with sweat in the early morning light. It was hot already, and the sun was just peeking over the trees behind the village. The well had a crossbar above it, and two ropes ran over the wooden post. Deep grooves had been worn into the wood, making it look like a piece of sculpture people would buy in America.

The two girls worked with a rhythm that made it look easy. I noticed the muscles in their backs under their smooth black skin, flinching with each pull. A sheen of sweat covered their torsos in the soft, early morning light. Their hands played leapfrog, one over the other, grabbing the rope and pulling up the water. When the bucket reached the top, the front girl snagged it and poured the water into the bucket of another girl. She didn't spill a drop.

The girl with the full bucket crouched down gracefully and put it on her head. She walked up to me and grinned, then strolled away like someone balancing a book on her head instead of a heavy, sloshing bucket of water.

I was really concentrating on looking everyone in the eye. Not because I was looking for meaningful communication, or whatever they had taught us in public speaking class. No. I was trying not to look at all the bare breasts around me. "Doesn't anyone feel embarrassed?" I wanted to ask Khadi. But how could I do that? She was dressed, or undressed, the same way!

Since I was a guest, the other girls let us have our water next. With just one smooth motion, Khadi lifted the full bucket to her head, not spilling a drop. Then taking my hand again, we walked back to the hut.

It was strange, but in California I would have rather

died than hold hands with Gina or Lisa. But in Bukama, having Khadi, who I could barely talk to, hold my hand as we walked past huts and goats, kids playing and men stretching in the golden morning light, seemed totally natural. Not geeky or weird or anything. Just good. Women smiled at us as we passed, calling out to Khadi things I couldn't understand. All I knew was that Khadi's hand gave me confidence in the strangest place I'd ever been.

She led me into the hut, where my mom was just hanging out in her hammock. She smiled at us as we came through the door, or I should say grinned, so I was pretty sure she was going to say something wise. She didn't fail me.

"Luk wi yu de swet!" she said. Khadi laughed. I didn't need an interpreter to know she was laughing at my sweaty face and sticky jeans.

"Good morning to you too," I said with a growl. My mom rolled from her hammock like the drops of sweat rolling off my chin. Seeing her do it so naturally made me wonder how many new things there were to learn about my mom.

In America she always knew what to do when, how to get anywhere, how to talk her way out of anything. I suddenly found myself wanting to show her that I was also the confident one. Watching her rise from the native hammock as naturally as the sun rises from the horizon, I realized just how difficult that would be. She was already so at home in our new surroundings.

She came over and put her arm around my sweat-slick shoulder, and I thought, *Now that is true love.* She squeezed me. "Don't worry, dear," she said, "it's not always this hot here. Come on, I'll show you how to take your first birdbath and wash some of this sweat off."

I bent to pick up the bucket Khadi had carried on her head like a pillow, and nearly wrenched my back. It weighed more than my suitcase. I could barely get it off the ground, and she had just walked ten minutes with it on her head like a model walking down a runway.

"Normally people don't wash inside the hut, but they'll let us," my mom told me.

"Well, if you think that someday I'll be out scrubbing it up in public, you're wrong there. BIG TIME."

Khadi cocked her head as if trying to understand what I'd said.

"Not to worry. Tomorrow you can use the little washing stall next to the long drop out back. We'll just bathe in here today so you can see how to do it." She put two large metal basins down on the dirt floor and stepped into one. "The trick is to see how little water you can use and still feel clean."

With a flip of her wrist she undid the lapa she was wearing, and it dropped next to the headpan, then she bent over and took off her underwear as if we did this kind of stuff together all the time—which we didn't.

Taking a half of a gourd hanging from the wall in front of her, she poured water over herself. "You get fourteen gourdfuls—seven to wash and seven to rinse." Then she counted as she poured water over each arm, each leg, down her front and back, and one for her head. "Remember, use as little water as possible." Khadi was still watching.

"No problem," I said. "I just saw what it takes to get a bucket of water. Believe me, I'll never waste another drop."

I was kind of stalling. Never did I expect to ever see my mother bathing. Especially standing starkers right in front of my face. Her back was to me, and I felt strange looking at my own mother's buns.

"Quit stalling," she said over her wet shoulder.

I hadn't noticed that Khadi had left until she came in again. She had a cloth over her arm and held it out to me. "Fo yu," she said simply, then turned and walked outside again. Somehow she knew this wasn't easy for me. I peeled my jeans off, figuring I'd have to do it sometime. I turned my back to my mom as I took off my clinging shirt, so we were facing opposite walls, but sharing the same bucket. She handed me the gourd, and when the first cool water ran down my back, I shivered with pleasure. I actually felt cold.

By the time we finished, there was still half a bucket of water. My mom looked in the bucket and said, "Not bad. By next week we'll only use a quarter of a bucket. Now you know why they call it a birdbath."

I was looking at the cloth Khadi had given me while my mom got all gooey about birdbaths. It was about three feet long with a design of big roosters in circles, bright orange on red and green. A lapa, I knew that.

"Do you want me to show you how to fix it?" my mom asked. "Remember your jeans yesterday?"

She was standing there, wrapped in the one she had used in Freetown and a T-shirt that said WILD WOMEN NEVER GET THE BLUES. Just like getting out of the hammock, she looked natural. "I notice you have a top on," I said.

She laughed. "Don't worry, dear, even I can't go totally local. It's interesting though. It's considered perfectly acceptable for a woman to bare her breasts, but not her legs. That means either you wear a lapa or long pants, so the sooner you get used to this, the better you'll feel. Shorts are definitely out."

Just then Khadi's head popped through the door again. Quickly I put on my going-away T-shirt from Felix, the one with bright green letters saying FELIX SEZS: HELLLLOOOO AFRICA!

My mom offered again to show me how to put on the lapa, but I wanted Khadi to. I wanted her to know that I wanted to fit right in. Be like her. She had accepted me as a friend faster than any kid in California. Faster than even Felix. And I wanted to show her that I had accepted her too.

"Please show me," I said, holding the lapa out to her. With one quick motion Khadi pulled the cloth around me from both sides, and quickly folded one end over the other, tucking them into opposite sides of my waist. I actually felt kind of dressed up in my long skirt. I also felt much cooler. The sweat could run down my legs and off, instead of my jeans soaking it up and sticking to me.

Figuring that the lapa was only step one in my transformation, I scooped up the bucket and put it on my head. It was much lighter half full, but when I set it on my head I felt my neck squinch down like a spring. Even with both hands on the bucket the water sloshed around. Both my mom and Khadi laughed at my surprised look.

Khadi took the bucket and gave me a small tin can instead. "Yu need fo start slow slow," she said. Then she said "Na bifo fut, na im bien fut de fala."

I looked at my mom for help and she told me, "She said, 'The back foot follows the front one.' What she means is little kids learn by copying their big sisters and brothers. They always start with tin cans rather than big buckets. I think you have a teacher, my dear, not to mention a friend."

And so began my classes. In carrying water on my head. In collecting firewood, and carrying that on my head. In cooking over a fire. We started working in the fields for hours, swinging hoes in time to the voices singing, laughing at the stories told through the songs. My Krio was coming together fast, which was probably bad, in the end, for I thought I knew everything since I could make a joke in Krio. In the end it was clear that I didn't know anything

8

"I HAD A GREAT DAY," SAID MY MOM AS SHE breezed in the door one evening. I was sitting on my bed, holding a flashlight in my mouth, shining it onto a sliver I was removing from my right hand. I had gotten it collecting the firewood that morning, and had to stop my schoolwork to pull it out because I couldn't write. When I looked up at my mom, the flashlight beamed onto her face, all smiles as she hugged her notebook to her breasts, like some dorky kid in love.

Spitting out the flashlight, I asked, "What was so great?" In that same moment the top half of the log lodged under my skin pulled free.

"Just come out and look," she said. "We'll remove the lumber from your hand later." We crossed the compound and stood on the top of a large slope that led down to the beach. It was good to walk beside my mom, who was gone most of each day. She always left before I was up to be with the women meeting the fishing boats.

"My work is going great," she had told me a week before. "I never knew, in those two years as a Peace Corps volunteer here, that different women do different jobs in the fishing business." Throwing her arms wide, she had said, "Some meet boats, others sell and others smoke the fish or dry it. But no woman sees a fish all the way through. That means I spend time with all the women from the village, which I really need to do."

"So do you actually do the work with them, or sit in the shade and take notes?"

"I work, believe me I do. It's the only way to get their respect and friendship. How would Khadi feel if you just watched her hoeing or washing clothes? She not only loves you, but she respects you too. I can see it."

I had glowed inside when my mom said that. "So what do you all talk about?"

"All kinds of things, but unfortunately not the thing I want to talk about most. That's why I've worked so hard for their respect these first weeks—in the fields and the market, on the beach. Maybe now I can get to it."

"What is 'it'?" I asked. I hadn't gotten into her work much. I had enough of my own to do.

"Tell you what, if 'it' becomes an issue, then I'll get to 'it' with you too. With any luck though, you won't have to know about 'it.' "

Sticking her hand up to stop me before I could argue, she said in separate, clear words, "End of topic."

"It" had been on my mind ever since, but when my mom put her arm across my shoulders that day as we strolled to the beach, I didn't bring it up. I wanted to enjoy the moment.

The sun was just setting, and the sky melted from blue to pink to fiery orange. Six women on the beach were gathered around a giant grill, the coals growing brighter as the dusk grew darker. Three were cleaning fish with single swipes of their blades and a flick of their wrists, tossing the guts aside. Snarling dogs fought over the bloody mess. Two other women threw the cleaned fish onto the sizzling grill. Laughter echoed across the beach as the sixth woman danced to music only she could hear, shaking her big bottom from side to side with her arms stretched high and wide over her head. The women laughed with glee as she started wrenching her pelvis back and forth in a frenzied way. One started clapping and the others joined, driving the beat faster and faster and the dancer's hips too. Her head lolled back, and she smiled toward the sky, shaking everything she had with total wild abandon.

"I just love it," my mom said again. "I mean, look at those women. Look at how happy they are, and think how little they have as we know it. How little they own.

What hardships they face keeping their kids healthy and food on the fire. What's that say to you?"

"It says sex to me," I said, pointing at the dancer who was slowing down and making little grunts. Her friends whooped and laughed and high fived each other as the dancer collapsed in a heap. Like all kids, I'd seen plenty of sex scenes in movies and knew that what the dancer was doing standing up I'd seen people do lying down. My mom was also big on talking about sex. "What you know can protect you," she'd always say.

Waving to the women, she said, "That's part of it, but mainly people just make their own fun. Life is tough, and still there's time to laugh at the end of a fourteen-hour workday. There's a joy to life here that I don't feel back home."

A billowing gray cloud rising off the grill brought all the women back to their job at hand, smoking the fresh fish for tomorrow's market. They elbowed one another to get closer to the grill, flipping the hot fish bare-handed.

"Look at them," my mom continued. "They look like they're at the beginning of their day instead of the end.

"We were all on this same beach at dawn, watching the fishing boats skim in across the waves. Since then we've bought fish, cleaned fish, sold fish, collected water, cooked meals, swept compounds, changed babies, scolded some naughty boys, washed clothes and bought more fish to smoke for tomorrow. And look at them, they're still dancing and laughing and having fun. We're looking at the backbone of Africa, Jodie—the women. They make sure their kids eat and they have school fees. And sad but true, they also watch them die from malaria and suffer from worms. But that's what makes them so great—they still find something to celebrate in the day."

"Can you shake it like that? I mean, do you do that with them too, or just all the work?" I had made a point of going my own way these first weeks, both for my mom's sake and my own. Our paths rarely crossed in a day, I was so busy with collecting wood, hoeing, getting water and being with Khadi that we usually met only at sunset. Then each night after dinner, she wrote her notes and I studied. "Can you?" I said again.

She put her hands on her hips and started shaking her butt side to side, turning small circles on her heel. "Stop!" I shouted, hoping no one else would see her acting so goofy. But the women on the beach looked up and started laughing and clapping and driving her on to further madness. She stretched her arms out from her sides and, bending at her waist, she lifted the edge of her lapa up her leg. The clapping increased, till she threw her head back and laughed, standing up straight.

"Yu know fo dance, Sistah Val!" one shouted at her, then they got back to their grill.

I grabbed my mother's arm and said, "Sistah Val, wi

need fo get you inside before the world de see ow yu de craze." As I dragged her along I couldn't help but be impressed with her wild dance, and happy that she was so happy. Africa brought something out in her that I never saw in California.

Her crazy mood carried on right through dinner and into a game of Crazy Eights with me by the light of our kerosene lamp. Sausage bugs with bloated bodies flew against the lamp's glass, falling to the floor as their wings fell off. We could hear a neighbor's radio tuned to *Voice of America* blasting some old rock-and-roll song. My mom sang along loudly. As she sang and shuffled, I pulled at a broken blister on the palm of my hand.

Underneath the dead skin was a pink sea of fresh flesh that stood out against the background of tough skin. My mom put down the cards and examined my hands.

"Not exactly baby-butt soft," I said as she held my palms up in the lamp's light.

She traced around the outside of the newly revealed skin and said, "Are you having fun, Jodie? These hands look like I brought you to Africa so I could work you to death."

"Yeah, I am," I said. "But there's just one thing that really has me confused. One day Felix was talking about the 'simple life.' I'm trying to figure out why, if simple means no electricity, no running water, no modern gizmos, it's so much more difficult. Seems to me that simple is supposed to be the opposite of difficult. And difficult is definitely the only way to describe life here. Nothing is simple. Unless maybe you've been doing it your whole life. Look what it takes just to pee! So what does the simple life mean?"

My mom threw back her head and laughed. "I love you, Jodie. Good question. Maybe simple refers to not having to choose which restaurant to go to, because there aren't any."

"Or maybe not having to pick a movie from a list of dozens, because there isn't even one to choose from," I added.

"Maybe it's supposed to be simple because you don't have any electricity bills to pay or no one can shut your water off," my mom said, laughing.

"No, I know. Simple means not fighting over the remote control!"

Just then an old Eagles song came on. My mom picked up her hairbrush and sang into it as if it were a microphone. With her eyes closed and her face scrunched I couldn't resist telling her, "I think I've got another definition for simple. You should see yourself."

She continued singing into her microphone as I got up. "Good night," I told her. "We weed the rice tomorrow so I'd better get to sleep. Oh yeah, thanks for the show."

* * *

EVERY DAY WAS THE SAME BUT DIFFERENT. WE went to the well first, for cooking and washing water. I had gotten the hang of hauling the water up and considered myself a pro at carrying it. Taking a spare lapa, I rolled it into a doughnut shape and placed it on my head. Bending from the knees, I swooped down and lifted my container, setting it on the doughnut.

Most days were spent working in the fields. Growing rice is a beautiful sight. It's planted in flat lands, shimmering green in the morning light, that have small walls built around them to keep water inside. The sun was brutal, reflecting in the water back to our faces. It had taken almost a month to get the field ready for planting.

I'll never forget the day Ma Luba came to the rice fields after a week of our hard work. With strong swipes of her razor-sharp panga, she cut several dried palm fronds on our way to the fields. We walked along a path through thick bush, chatting and laughing along the way. Our fifteen-minute walk ended at a large, grassy area. I thought Ma Luba was going to build a shade shelter or something with the fronds. Instead, she bunched two long, dry ones together and lit the ends. I lost it when she started walking around with the flaming torches, setting fire to the tall grass.

"Wetin yu du?" I screamed and grabbed Ma Luba's arm. Everything got quiet.

Khadi moved next to me and tried to pull my hand off Ma Luba's arm. She said, "Du ya, Ah beg," to Ma Luba as she tried to lead me away with a strong yank. Ma Luba looked at me like I'd lost my last marble.

"Na wetin yu go make palaver fo?" she asked me. Her jaw was rigid and looked like wet ebony. She shook her arm loose and lit another fire.

"Stop!" I screamed, and tried to grab her again. I couldn't believe that she was setting fires, especially so close to the village. Pictures of L.A. in the fire season swept through my head. A raging fire is dangerous. Felix's grandmother had lost her house in a fire a year ago. She never did recover from the shock of it all. Her sad face flashed through my head as Ma Luba stuck her flames to another stand of tall weeds.

"Mud huts won't burn, but thatch roofs will," I yelled at her. Except for the crackling of the fire, it was silent. Everyone stared at me.

"Wi need fo burn to clean the land," Khadi said to me in the crackling silence. Her head hung down in embarrassment.

"That's crazy!" I was breaking all the rules screaming at Ma Luba, but I wasn't thinking. "Why don't we just cut the grass? I'm sure you've been doing it this way for years, and I'm sure you don't want to change," I yelled, turning to Khadi and the other women, "but I'm here to tell you that people don't go around setting fires to make your work easier."

My Krio had completely failed me in my outburst, so Khadi translated to the women who didn't speak English. While Khadi talked, Ma Luba handed her flaming branches to Sistah Honoria. Then she walked over to her headpan that had her lunch and her panga in it. The three-foot blade glinted in the sun as she picked it up. With a look at me that could dry plums into prunes in no time, she walked past me.

Khadi's voice wound down, as we all watched Ma Luba. She cut four pegs of wood from a branch she had collected on the way to the fields. With silent determination she marked out a square in the grass. Watching me like a cat watches a mouse, she slowly walked over to me.

"Dis be yu field," she said, pointing to the place she'd just marked. Then she turned and faced the rest of the rice field. Sweeping her arm right to left, she pointed at the land as big as two or three football fields. "Dat be we field."

She handed me the panga and said, "Yu de clean poo-mui way, wi de clean Mende way. Wi see which side go finish furst." She collected the burning palm frond from her co-wife, Sistah Honoria, and went back to setting fires.

All right then, I would. I planted both feet in "my field." My first swing of the panga only ruffled the grass like a strong wind. I swung the panga back and forth trying hopelessly to cut the tall, bending grass.

"Yu need fo reech down like so, not-a-so?" said Khadi as she grabbed a bunch of grass in one hand and cut it with her other down by the roots.

Ma Luba looked our way and shouted at Khadi, "Lef her. She de work alone, and show us her poo-mui ways."

I realized Khadi was getting into trouble for my sake, and thanked her silently for giving me the clue of how to cut the grass. Determined to show them, I bent in half, one hand holding the tall scratchy grass and the other slashing the shiny panga. The sun burnt down on my bent back, and my arms itched like wildfire, scratched by the tall grasses. I expected to be bitten by a snake any minute, and thought, *Let them explain that to my mom.* My face, the red of a ripe tomato, pulsated with my heartbeat. The women sang as they set fires, then went and sat in the shade of a big old cotton tree.

Their field, fifty times bigger than mine, was done before the sun dipped toward the horizon. As they gathered their headpans and lapas, Ma Luba came over to me.

She took in my stoplight face and drenched T-shirt and said, "Cum. Wi de go jus now."

There was nothing I wanted more than to quit, but I couldn't. I looked at her and said, "Yu done done firs today, but wi go see if fast cleaning get da best rice later. Ah need for finish. Wi go see." *At least I hadn't risked the village*, I thought to myself. I turned my back on her and continued slashing the grass.

She clapped her hands and laughed at me. "Yu tink yu woman, but yu jus big pikin like big baby."

She put her pan on her head and started back to the village, singing a song about the crazy poo-mui who likes to make work. She grabbed Khadi's left elbow and started her walking, making sure she didn't stay behind to help. Khadi looked at me over her shoulder as she left. The sad look in her eye wasn't hard to read. It was as clear as her missing smile. She just shook her head and shrugged, then flipped me a little wave good-bye with her free right hand.

I dragged into the village just before dark. My mom was sitting under the mango tree with Ma Luba and several other women. Their conversation stopped as I drew near. My mom stood, and took my shoulder like a cop arresting a crook. We didn't talk all the way to our hut. In fact, we didn't talk at all until after dinner.

My back ached beyond words, and my hands were a mass of blisters, but I wasn't going to let anyone know. When I put my hands into the bucket of soapy water to wash our dishes, I gasped. The soap stung like ten thousand little knives as it hit my raw-meat hands.

My mom came over and pulled them from the water.

She winced slightly and said, "Maybe you've already learned your lesson."

I couldn't believe it. I looked at her, my eyes bugging in amazement and said, "Excuse me? Did you forget who your daughter is in this, your wounded daughter? Mercy no de."

"That's for sure. Especially no mercy for rude young women. And if you want to talk about wounded, let's talk about Ma Luba. Young girls do not shout at older women. In fact, they do as they're told when they're told. And they show respect to their elders. Always."

My mom pulled her suitcase out from under her bed, then opened it to find our first-aid kit. "It's probably my fault because I let you get away with a lot, say what you want to say. But you will apologize to her tomorrow, in front of everyone that was there today, for embarrassing her."

"Apologize for shouting?" I asked.

"For starters," she said. "And for glaring at her, 'like a snake with bad intentions,' as she calls it. And for turning your back on her as if she didn't exist. Jodie, it's not acceptable in their culture, and I've just decided that it's not acceptable in our culture either. From now on you'll treat all your elders with respect, or you'll spend all your time alone, in this hut."

"But Mom, they were burning up the land. What about Smokey the Bear and Girl Scouts and everyone else who ever said don't light fires? What about Felix's grandmother, poor old Mrs. Warren? Just to save a little time you torch the land? In America . . ."

"That's part of the problem, Jodie," she cut right in. "This isn't America, and you don't have all the answers. If you'd asked, they would have explained why they burn. It's fast, but it's also good for the land. It gets rid of the insects that would eat their seedlings. And it lets loose nutrients in the soil that the rice needs. It's not laziness, Jodie, and it's not your place to say it is, even if it was. So tomorrow you'll apologize. Now let's do something about these hands."

I tossed and turned most of the night, thinking about what I would say. I was embarrassed now. Not because I had yelled or fought for something I believe in, but because I was wrong. And not only wrong—I'd even made a challenge about who would grow the best rice. I winced, remembering my mom saying, "And the quality and quantity of rice they get is always better from the burned fields." I groaned out loud.

The next morning I bit the bullet when we were all gathered under the mango tree, and said to Ma Luba in front of Khadi and all the others, "Du ya, Ah beg. Ah wan fo say sorry-o. Dis one poo-mui which talk too too much and too too big."

She came over to shake my hand and jumped when

I jerked it away. Gently she took my hands and turned them over. The skin almost looked like the face of the moon with craters and bumps, except it was too red to be the moon. She smoothed her fingers over the mess, saying, "Oh sha," then took me to a plant growing in front of a nearby hut. It looked like a cactus with long rubbery leaves. She broke one off and a clear gooey sap oozed out. She carefully dribbled it across my palms, and it felt like a cooling breeze on a hot day. "Dis be aloe," she said. "Yu be fine-o quick quick."

As Khadi and I walked home that afternoon she took me through a small forest I'd never seen before. A huge, round rock, smooth to the touch, sat like a king on a throne in the center of a round, cleared spot.

Putting my hand on the rock, Khadi said, "Ah de come here when Ah lose sense. When Ah de talk rubbish or get confusion, Ah de come here and touch jus lek so." She released my hand and rubbed hers up and down and over and across the smooth, speckled surface of the round rock. "Na soon Ah feel fine-o."

I felt so bad I hugged the rock with my whole body. My legs pressed tight from the thigh to the ankle and my arms wrapped as far as they could reach. As I hugged, I asked, "Is it true? Burned fields get better rice?"

She nodded yes, then said, "Jodie, Ah no able fo understand. All my life, Ah de do wetin de elders tell me.

But yu, yu no lissen for no side. Yu jus axs questions lek so, and yell. Ah no de gree. Yu need fo lissen some some time. Ah done bring yu inside my most favorite spot, most restful place for dis talk wi talk. Du ya, Ah beg, take time."

I thought about what she said. "Okay, Ah de gree. Ah de craze too much. Ah go fo control from dis day forward. But Ah need fo say jus one ting, thank ya pas words fo bringin me to your place. Ah be too gladdie."

My hands healed in no time, and thanks to Khadi, my pride did too. I tried never to assume anything again, especially where work was concerned. Six weeks after planting the rice it was time to weed. I looked at my healed hands, then at the green plants, rice and weeds. "Sistah, which be rice na which be weed? I no sabe." All the long green plants looked alike to me.

"Yu go lek so," Khadi told me as she yanked a green weed up. It was just about the same color as the rice, but it didn't have a pointy little head like the rice does.

The women sang and called back and forth while we worked. I laughed at a song Ma Luba was singing about a poo-mui busting her chops in a field of rice.

Jodie Jodie, poo-mui pickin
in de nem of God
Chop chop chop, pull pull pull
till yu face get red lek kola nut, red dat shine

Jodie Jodie, poo-mui pickin
in de nem of God, Ah de say,
Du ya, Ah beg, rest!

Salimatu and Njai fell against each other laughing, losing the beat they were banging on their lunch pans. I knew my red face glowed with pride. My mom had told me that the work songs were always about people they like, and so I felt good as they sang about me. Khadi was at my side, singing and laughing like all the rest, and I thought, *I really do finally fit in somewhere.*

9

LATE ONE AFTERNOON, AS THE SUN SHONE through the leaves of the trees, Khadi and I were down at the stream that runs behind the village, washing clothes. We stood in water almost knee deep, pounding lapas and tank tops, underwear and headties against a large rock that had been worn smooth with time and use. As we worked, Khadi sang in a voice as clear as a songbird, and we washed to the beat of her song.

Fatima, Khadi's youngest sister, rushed down to the water, waving something above her head as she ran. The usual group of kids looking for action followed behind her, pushing and shoving, laughing and yelling. Fatima, feeling very important, called to me, "Jodie, cum out and get yu letta. It jus now reech from America."

I shot from the stream like a torpedo. As I snatched the letter I realized just how much I wanted mail. For weeks I'd wandered past Pa Ponta, the village postman.

His shoulders were broad like a fisherman, but one arm ended in a sudden stump and it was clear that he hadn't hauled in a net for years. Without me saying a word, he'd wave his stump at me and call, "Today mail no de, but tamara mail maybe de. Na God willing na Inshallah. When it come, I de send it just lek so," as he slammed his arm against his thigh. For almost two months we had this conversation over and over again.

"YES! MAIL!" I shouted as I took the letter. The envelope was dirty, with the fingerprints of many people on it. Felix's name, followed by the face of a smiling cat, was on the outside. It was my first letter from him.

Quickly I sat upon the rock we had been working against and tore open the envelope. The letter was five paragraphs long, each written in a different color of ink.

Dear Jodie,

Thanks for your letter, my first from Africa. I have to tell you, give me the sweat and flies and heat anytime, for here life is just its same old boring self.

Lisa has now decided that she'll have three kids rather than two. Gina is organizing the class prom. And I am just pondering the important questions in life, like "Is it true wet birds never fly at night?"

Your friend Khadi sounds great. It seems like someone who was scared about going to Africa is doing pretty well there. (Did you really think I couldn't tell you were scared, even if you didn't say so?) I am jealous of you, and the adventures you're having.

Could you ask your mom if there's anything she left behind that she needs? Tell her I can bring it to her. Or if you need anything, I can bring it to you. I can't imagine you getting water from a well or carrying a bucket on your head. You must have some killer muscles by now.

Well Jodie, keep writing me those great letters. I love to sweat and groan with you. Actually, I am going to use them for a social studies project. I'll call it, "An Outsider's View of Africa." I'll write a short introduction about you and where you are, then put in your letters. This way I'll write two pages and you'll write twenty. You'll be doing my homework for me! Pretty cool, huh? Really though, I look forward to hearing from you again, toot sweet. That's French for right now. You're not the only one learning a new language.

With love, not I love you, your friend, Felix

When I finished reading I looked up and saw Khadi watching me carefully. I could feel the giant smile covering my face, and a nice warm feeling wandering slowly through my body. It felt great to feel connected with Felix for a minute, especially at such a great distance.

"He signed it 'love,' " I said with a breathy voice.

Khadi was holding the envelope, turning it slowly in

her hands, then she pressed it to her chest. "Yu want fo leave us now?" she asked worriedly.

"Heck no," I said. "Wetin mek yu ask me so?"

She took the letter from my hands and held it upside down. Her eyes, usually so clear and certain, had a foggy haze across them. She tilted her head to one side, and asked shyly, "Is hard fo mek letta like so?"

"No," I said, "just get some paper and a pen, and get to it. Most people just write in one color, but not Felix. He never does anything like anyone else."

She turned the letter in her hands like someone trying to find the top of a map. Suddenly I realized that I'd never seen Khadi read. In fact I'd never seen her with a book or a newspaper in her hands, but I'd seen plenty of other people in the village reading. Mainly men, when I stopped to think about it. I just figured I never saw Khadi reading because she was always too busy doing something else, like cooking a meal or chopping wood. Now a new thought popped into my head.

"Go ahead and read it," I said. It was a rotten thing to do, but I didn't know if it was worse just to outright ask her if she could read and write.

She shoved the letter back at me and said, "Yu de fala makata mi." In one motion she swept up her headpan of wash and stomped away. I could see tiny fish scatter in the wide wake she left behind.

I jumped off the rock and ran after her. "I'm not mocking you," I said. "I just didn't know if it is rude to ask someone if they can read or write. Ah beg padin, du ya, Ah beg," I said. I had made more apologies in Sierra Leone then I'd made in my first fourteen point three years of life. Did that mean I was growing up? Or did it mean I was getting less sure of myself? I didn't know. But it worked.

Khadi stopped on the path from the washing rock. She shifted her headpan to her hip, and plopped her other hand on her other side.

Before she could say a word I blurted out, "Wait, this is perfect. I always wondered how I could ever do for you what you've done for me. You know, repay you?"

She took a few steps down the sandy path toward me, so I said, "I'm sure you'll come to America one day, and what can I teach you about survival there? How to turn on the TV? Or load the dishwasher? Possibly how to drive? Things that you'll never use at home? I'll probably always carry my backpack on my head when I get home after carrying everything from water to firewood to bananas here.

"But now I know, Khadi. Don't you see? I'll teach you to read and write. It be de best best gift, one sistah to her finest sistah. Please let me—du ya?"

I was out of breath when I finished, and didn't know how much she had understood, but it was clear she'd gotten the message. Her eyes were wide like a doll's, and they shined in the sunlight. I could see my reflection in the deep dark pools of her pupils as she reached for the lapa I was wringing to death.

"Yu no de lie?" she asked. "Yu no fo talk foolishness? Yu mean fo du it jus like so?" She reached over and grabbed my hand. She traced each finger with hers, a sure sign she was excited.

"Na tru. Wi go lan yu. Everyday after we finish duin wi work tings. I'll even teach yu while wi work."

Khadi dropped her headpan with a thunk onto the sand, and grabbed me by my shoulders. "Wi able fo start jus now?" she asked me as her grip tightened in excitement.

"Jus now. Repeat after me, A, B, C, D, E, F, G."

"AB—CD—EFG," she said. "Wetin dat mean? Ah wan fo lan readin an writin, Ah know how fo sing."

"No, it's your letters. The alphabet. You can't read till you know them. So class begins jus now."

During the next weeks, then months, we weeded, hoed, washed clothes, cut wood, pulled water and shelled peanuts to the alphabet. In no time, Khadi was writing anyone's name who wanted it and short sentences. She was also reading her youngest brother's English schoolbooks. Khadi, the oldest girl in her family, had three older brothers and two younger ones who all went to school. But not Khadi, or her little sister Fatima, or most other girls in the village. Khadi was too busy working in the fields and helping her mother cook and wash. Even with such a long day, reading and writing were two things she just couldn't get enough of.

"Ah need for make small money," she told me one day.

"Wetin for?" I asked her.

She led me down to the sea where the women grill fish, and set to work cleaning the grill and getting the fire going. As she scrubbed the wire grill with the stringy insides of a coconut husk, she said, "Ah de make ready the fire for ten ten cents after de sell de fish."

"But wetin yu need money fo? Ah de get ten ten cents. Wetin yu need so bad?"

"Candles," she said.

"Candles?" I echoed. "Birthday cake candles?"

It was her turn to look confused, so she said shyly, "Candles fo read."

"Do you read every night?" I knew she was tired most nights after her busy day.

"Ah de read every chance," she said with pride.

Khadi was feeling proud and looking so, and I felt proud of her. And of me in a way too, for I saw someone change from the best gift I had ever given. We had studied hard together for these days and weeks—in the fields, on the beach, at the river and on Sundays under the shade of the mango tree. And now Khadi could read. And write. Those were definitely the happiest months of my life at the village, and I spoiled it all.

10

THUNDER ROLLED DOWN THE BEACH ONE evening, and then rolled into Bukama. Dark clouds reared across the sky like stallions on the run. The wind charged back and forth, changing directions in sudden violent gusts, leaving frothy trails on the ocean's surface. Dust devils danced across the place where the dirt meets the beach, and finally, the sky sat on the village.

From one dark cloud blocking out the setting sun, sheet lightning shot, then thunder surrounded the village. I screamed as the intense sound shook my bones, and ran for the hut. The rain came, big plopping drops that dug small craters upon landing on the dusty, parched earth. The trees bent with the winds, and the raindrops hit me from all different angles.

Khadi came running across the compound, arms outstretched wide and spun little circles around me. My face streamed with the cooling, fresh liquid that slithered down my head and under the neckline of my tank top. Khadi, bare-breasted as usual and dripping wet, looked like a picture out of an art book. We had waited months for the first real rain, and the "weather pas cold," Khadi insisted, was coming. Mud stuck to the back of my calves as I joined Khadi in her circle dance.

We hugged, then she threw back her head and shouted, "Ah de say Tank Ya God. Yu de be too too merciful!"

No sooner had the rain started then it ended. The clouds, still moving with the whipping winds, moved inland and left behind a stillness hard to describe. The sky was a collage of pastels, like an artist's well-used palette, and there was a light that gave everything a new sharpness and clarity. The muted browns and greens of the dusty plants and the huge old mango tree suddenly shined. Everything looked brand new.

"Dis go be one fine fine night," Khadi said.

"Dis jus now be fine fine," I replied, soaking up the sudden beautiful colors.

She wrung the water from the end of her lapa, "Na tru. But more dan de rains go start tonight. Wi go see, Ah need fo prepare."

I assumed she meant go prepare dinner, but I learned again, just like in the rice field, never assume anything.

Shortly after sunset, a full moon rose behind the village. I sat leaning against a coconut tree overlooking the beach. "Felix, you'd love it," I said under my breath. The moon was a disc that glowed with an attitude. It was bright and yellow and as round as a shiny silver dollar. Long tree shadows fell along the ground, all pointing at the beach. And suddenly the air, so fresh and clear from the rain, filled with the loudest, most strident drumbeats I'd ever heard.

I turned to find Ma Mary, usually a quiet woman with a serious face and style, come walking from the opposite side of the village into the moonlight. She had her head tied in an elaborate gold scarf, and wore a pile of twenty or thirty necklaces dangling down between her breasts. Her lapa was cinched tightly around her waist with a snakeskin belt, but what really surprised me was the drum.

Shaped like a large bowl with a very narrow bottom, it hung from her neck. She flipped open the front of her lapa and placed a foot on her opposite knee. She whipped the drum into the spot her legs and foot made and began to beat with wild abandon. As the beat got faster, she began to turn circles on her other foot, the newly rained-on ground forming little ridges of mud as she swirled.

Women poured out of the space between Ma Luba's and Pa Jalloh's huts. The first four women beat drums that looked like long tubes of thick bamboo. Twenty more women wearing thick grass skirts and ankle shakers made of tiny tomato paste cans filled with stones, followed them. Each woman carried firewood. They danced into a circle, legs stamping hard on the ground, and all heads bent as if watching their feet.

I was surprised to see an old woman I didn't know enter the circle and drop her firewood. One by one they all did the same. Then Ma Jalloh entered the circle with a flaming torch and set the wood on fire. As the flames grew, the dancing got faster, and the drummers leapt with their own beats. It was like everyone saw a sign that only I missed, for the drums suddenly stopped as one and so did the dancers. Bang! Finished! *How did they do that?* I wondered.

Women swooned from the dancing, and three of the drummers leaned against friends. Ma Mary, lapa closed and standing on two legs again, began beating a staccato beat on her drum, taptaptaptaptap. All talking stopped and the circle opened on the other side.

I was standing behind three tall men, so I elbowed my way forward as a space opened up in the front of the building crowd. I didn't know it was Khadi at first sight, for the whole scene was so bizarre it took a moment to register. She led a winding line of fourteen dancing girls into the circle. Each was slicked down with oil and carried a brightly colored umbrella. It was a stunning sight, these young budding black beauties, as my mother liked to call them, shining in the firelight and dancing under red, green and blue umbrellas.

There was so much energy there, in the girls and the women and the crowd that had gathered. I could feel it press in on me, but all I could think of was, *This is a Khadi I don't know.* I tried to catch her eye each time she danced past, but she was too caught up in what was going on to even see me. They danced until the drummer's arms gave out, then the circle of fire and light opened again and the young dancers left.

As I stared off after them, I saw my mother. I should have known. She was across the circle, near to where the girls passed, and her face was as elated and happy as all the others around her. I knew I didn't look happy. I had this strange feeling that everything was going to change. That this dance wasn't a one-time thing.

As I walked back to the hut I felt as if I was the only person in the village not smiling or jabbering or carrying on. Then I saw my mom again, walking with one arm around Ma Luba's shoulders and the other arm supporting a baby hooked to her hip, talking quietly in the moonlight. I watched her from a distance, amazed again that this was my California mother. The only thing that made it clear she wasn't born here was the color of her skin. Her walk was different—much more relaxed. And she laughed more than I'd seen her do all my life. But as I watched her with Ma Luba I could tell she was really feeling serious. Her worry lines were back around her mouth, and she'd completely lost that joyous look I'd seen just minutes before. *Why did she change so fast?* I wondered.

We reached the hut at the same time. I held the lapa aside for her to go in first, and when she sat by the kerosene lamp I could see sadness and anger in her eyes.

"What's it all about, Mom? Did you see Khadi out there? She looked like she'd left the planet. And running around dancing all topless and everything. I mean, come on. Mom, what is going on? Is this 'it'?"

My mom hunched down into her shoulders, then tilted her head up to look at me. With a strange absence of emotion in her voice, she said, "Secret Society, Jodie. Stay away from it.

"It's all about reaching puberty by popular demand, or command, I should say. I was really praying it wouldn't happen the year we're here, but it's here. It's what I was alluding to some weeks ago. I can't believe I didn't know it was going to happen tonight, but it just goes to show how secret the society is."

She rearranged the two unlit candles on either side of the lamp. "I spend all day with the women, and I never had a clue. I can't believe that for a while out there I was clapping and shaking and hey-hey-heying with the best of them, until I realized what it all meant.

"But I can't talk about it tonight, Jodie. I'm too distressed and frustrated. Tomorrow, I promise, we'll talk tomorrow." Then she rose slowly from her chair, placed it very carefully under the table with unusual precision, then turned, took one step and fell onto her bed. "Tomorrow Jodie, but tonight I just want to check out."

She closed her eyes as I dropped her mosquito net around her, and gave a low, " 'Night, honey." I stopped, thinking, *Uh-oh, there's that word—honey.* It stuck in my mind while I did my nightly snake checks under the beds and behind the one crooked, wooden cupboard in the room, on my knees and with my flashlight.

Lying in the dark, listening to my mother toss and turn, I suddenly remembered, or maybe heard for the first time, Khadi's words after the rain. "But more dan de rains go start tonight." Then I thought about my mom—and "it." Secret Society? What did that mean? And why did it make my mom so unhappy?

The next morning was the first time Khadi disappeared.

My mom was already gone when I awoke. Usually she woke me for a good-bye, but not this morning. "Guess she's still not ready to talk," I said to no one. Fixing myself a bowl of rice with peanut sauce for breakfast, I thought about the night before. What was I going to say to Khadi? I mean, I was really embarrassed. I thought I'd accomplished a lot getting over the bare-breast stuff in normal, day-to-day life. But dancing? In public? All greased up? With men there? And boys?

There was only one way to know—go talk to her. But

she was nowhere to be found. Her Auntie Sarah, sorting shiny red kola nuts into piles according to size, shrugged and said, "Ah no sabe which side she be," then quickly started a conversation with a passing old ma. Khadi's cousin, Joko, usually more than happy to talk with me, only said, "Me. Ah be ignorant." As he zoomed off like a man with a pressing appointment, I shouted at his back, "Ifn yu see her, say Ah want fo see her. Quick, quick."

The morning dragged. I chopped wood by myself, and collected water with girls half my age. Finally I decided to study so I wouldn't notice how lonely and anxious I felt. Khadi had never left me out of anything before. For 123 days we had been together, all day, carrying water, collecting firewood, washing clothes, sorting peanuts—you name it, we did it. Together. So where was she? No one that I asked wanted to talk to me about it. Her little brother, Bobo, rolled the wire ring he was playing with away from me. Finally I saw my mom at lunch, which was most unusual.

"Well?" I asked over leaf sauce and rice. We had moved our chairs out into the sunshine beside our hut. Wasting no time, I said, "So what about 'it'?"

She tried to swallow her words but they fell out too fast, "You look like you just lost your best friend . . ."

"Do you know where she is? We never go anywhere without each other. No one seems to know where she's gone, or any of the other dancing girls either, now that I think about it. Mom, why would she leave me out? We are best friends. Is her being gone connected to last night? Is it connected to 'it'?"

My mom busied herself with getting the last grains of rice off her spoon. "So where is she?" I said, for something told me that my mom knew. Just like Auntie Sarah and Joko and Bobo did.

"Jodie, Khadi will probably disappear a lot in the near future. It's the Secret Society I mentioned last night."

"What do you mean 'disappear'?" I asked.

"Well, she'll be joining a special age group for girls in the village. It's not anything you need to concern yourself with. No, let me say that a different way, it's off limits to you and me. A place where poo-muis cannot go."

"Off limits?"

"Yes. Definitely. Absolutely. It's called the Secret Society, Jodie, and that's the way they plan to keep it. Secret. Remember, every person in this village knew that dance was coming last night—except for you and me. That just shows the power of the Secret Society. So please stay away from it. It's taboo."

Taboo? Forbidden? Something I wasn't to touch!

Even though I always expected not to be included in everything, I could feel my jaw harden as I got angry at the idea of Khadi joining a club without me. Expecting and experiencing were two different things. When Khadi finally showed up late that afternoon, she had her hair in a new style, two fat pigtails sticking out of each side of her head. A wide, beaded headband held her hair in place, and she wore a huge flowered bra, with pointed cups that could poke your eyes out. Her arms and shoulders and body were covered in shiny oil. Two other girls, Njai and Salimatu, had the same 'do and bras. Identical, they all three were.

Khadi smiled at me, then came over and took my hand. "Cusheo, ow di bodi?" she asked.

She acted as if she wasn't standing there in pigtails and a Madonna look-alike bra. Like nothing had changed. If she can pretend, so can I. "Ah well, tank God," I said.

She had this glow about her, something words can't explain. I felt not only dull, but also tarnished next to her. And jealous. Yes, jealous. She looked like some super woman in a kid's fairy tale. Healthy. Pretty. Powerful.

"Ah want bad, pas words, to join yu club. Du ya, Ah beg," I spilled out before I knew it.

Her eyes flew open in shock, and she started to back away. "Yu no fo able. Yu no be Mende. Chance no de." Then she just walked away from me, like I didn't even exist.

As she stomped across the compound, I said to myself, "Chance no de, huh?"

11

WE MET AT THE WELL EARLY THE NEXT morning. Khadi was trying to balance her bucket between the two bulging pigtails, and I was carrying Ma Jenny's baby tied to my back. I held each little foot in the palms of my hands. Khadi nearly dropped her bucket when she saw me, calling out, "Yu get pikin last night?" A big smile lit her face.

"Ah no get pikin, but Ma Jenny get backache pas words. She de dance too much? Or drum too much?" I was hinting at the day before, the day I wasn't invited to the bush. The baby squirmed against my back, so I started bouncing lightly, and reached around to pat his snug little butt like I'd seen the women do. "Ah able fo join yu at de next dance. Ah tink Ah be ready fo lan dance jus now."

For months Khadi had been offering to teach me to dance like her, but I never did take her up on it. Shaking my butt in front of a crowd didn't appeal to me, but

I was feeling desperate. I was willing to try just about anything, except dancing topless.

Khadi knew immediately that I wasn't just talking about learning to dance. "Yu no able fo join Sande. Ah de say like so yesterday. Na lef it, du ya, Ah beg." With a major push she squeezed the bucket between her pigtails and left.

I told her parting back, under my breath, "Maybe."

Khadi and I had talked about everything, I thought, until the Secret Society came along. Then we talked about it—once.

We were walking single file to the rice field three mornings later. As we went, Khadi tried to explain to me the secrecy surrounding Sande, but it was difficult. I watched her muscles tense as we walked along, the strange sight of a big white bra crossing her usually empty back. She was strutting, and had little patience for my questions. She had never questioned the Secret Society. It was something she learned from her grandmother and would pass on to her granddaughters.

Completely forgetting my promise of months before to not be a know-it-all, I blurted out, "But you can't just believe it all. Just because they tell you to? You've got to ask some questions and get some answers. In America—"

Khadi stopped on the trail, and I crashed into her. Turning back to face me, she cut right in, something she'd never done before. "Dis no be America. Why," she asked, "yu get no respect fo the knowledge of the elders? Ow is it, yu na pikin still, sabe so much more dan anyone else? Yu need fo stop all dese questions about Sande jus now. Ah be patient, but no one else will be like so. Why yu wan fo look fo trouble, Jodie? Big big trouble. It be taboo fo talk like so about the Society with outsiders. So du ya, Ah beg, and stop humbugging me wit questions." Just like the day before, she turned around and stomped away.

That was the longest speech I ever heard Khadi make, and the second time in as many hours somebody used the word "taboo." But still, I didn't listen.

That night, sitting in a pleasant quiet, filled only with the far-off mindless barking of a village dog, I thought about Khadi and the Secret Society. My mom's head was bent in the shadow of the lantern hanging from the ceiling as she crouched close to write her notes. I dropped the sorted, dried beans into the pan from a higher and higher point trying to "accidentally" catch my mom's attention. The plunk of the beans on metal jarred in the warm silence that surrounded us. Finally my mom lifted her head and said, "What's on your mind, Jodie?"

I took a deep swallow, "How strong is taboo? I mean, what can happen if you break a taboo?"

My mom's face darkened like a cloud had passed between us. She reached across the table and pinned my hands to the smooth board. "Jodie, STAY AWAY from the Secret Society. You are not only not welcome—you are forbidden. Do you understand?"

"But what's the big secret? What goes on?" I said, trying to wriggle my hands free.

"Most of it is secret, Jodie, so we don't really know."

"But do you have an idea?" I persisted, finally working my hands out from under hers. "You've studied the women. You must know something."

"Yes, I have a very good idea about what goes on. They start with teaching the girls basic things like how to care for a husband, and the ways of loving a man. They learn about having babies and weaving and dancing, and how to squeeze thirty hours of work into a twenty-four-hour day." A slight breeze blew the candle flame into a dance, sending waving shadows along the mud wall.

In a voice that sounded like a frightened whisper, she continued. "Sorry to say, that's the good part. There's more to it than just learning how to treat a husband, and that's why I'm telling you to stay away from it. I mean it, Jodie."

"But why? Just because you say so?" I wanted some answers. Taboo is a major word. The ultimate no-no, and I wanted to know why.

"That should be reason enough, but knowing you and

your ways it's probably not enough. So how about be-cause they circumcise the girls?"

"Circumcise? That's what they do to baby boys. I don't get it. What do you mean they circumcise girls?"

My mom stretched across the scarred table, inches from my face. Her anger muscles twitched in her jaw as she said, "They cut the girls, Jodie. They cut off a small part of the girls'—"

I blurted out, "You mean the . . ." and pointed down there, to, well, to my crotch.

"Exactly," she said with a crisp nod and a disappear-ing mouth as she sucked her lips into a grim thin line. Just then a fruit bat flying over dropped a mango on a tin roof. I jumped as a loud, tinny BANG rang out. Dogs started barking everywhere.

"So what's that mean?" I asked, unable to stop myself, even though I was sure I didn't want to know.

"Besides a helluva lot of pain and high rates of terri-ble infections? It can also mean sterility, as well as mak-ing sure that the woman never has any pleasure during sex."

I looked at the hard-packed mud floor because I hate it when my mom gets talking about sex. Back home she'd talk about it all day if I let her, making little com-ments about how important the right partner is and how there's no need to rush into it. I knew more about AIDS than most doctors. Before she could launch into another sex lecture I asked, "Do you die from this circumcision stuff?"

My mom looked old. The candle sent a light across half her face, and there were suddenly wrinkles and a sad, far-away look in her eyes. Doodling a large knife in the top margin of her notes, she said, "You can. And they do. That's why I've avoided the subject, why I prayed that we were out of the cycle for this. I'm sorry, my mistake, because now it's here."

"But Khadi . . ." I jumped up and slammed the tabletop, knocking the flickering candle over onto her notes. "I won't let her be circumcised," I shouted, and ran for the door.

As I bolted for the door, my mom was like a professional ballplayer, swooping up the candle with one hand and grabbing my arm with the other. She yanked my arm like never before until I was on my knees, eye to eye with her.

In a whisper that filled each corner of our tiny hut, she hissed, "Jodie, stay out of it. It's not Khadi's choice, but it is her time." Each word sounded as if it was carved in stone.

"She can't choose whether to live or die?" I asked.

"Khadi is of this village. This is her world. She cannot choose whether or not to be a 'woman.' If she's not circumcised, and believe me, everyone will know, she'll never be married in this place." Shaking her head in disbelief she said, "And people won't even eat food she'll cook. She'll become an outsider in her own village."

"So she should risk dying?" I asked with a sneer creeping into my voice.

"Technically, yes, if she was to refuse."

"Technically? What the hell does that mean?" I tried to stand up but my mom yanked my arm again. Her face was inches from mine, and it was blotching into strange red puddles of color. I wasn't sure if that was because I had just sworn for the first time in front of her, or because of our fight.

Her eyes were as hard as Ma huba's in the rice field, and her voice brittle. "You must stay away, Jodie, and leave Khadi alone." Each word was short and sharp, like mangos hitting a metal roof. "Don't you see, if you interfere they . . . might come after *you*. Oh, Jodie, what if they tried to cut *you*!"

I slumped down below into the darkness beneath the table top. My knees were aching from squatting next to my mom, but she wouldn't let go of me.

"So it's all right for Khadi to get cut, but not me?" My shaking voice filled the hut.

"Oh, Jodie, of course it's not all right, but our culture isn't theirs, and changing things like this takes time."

"Well Mom, I hate to say it, but Khadi doesn't have time." I gave my arm a sudden jerk and leapt free.

As I ran for the door again, my mom barked out in a

voice I'd never heard before, something I thought they only say in movies, "If you go out that door then I'll start packing to leave—right now."

As I swept the lapa aside that keeps out the bats, I stopped dead in my tracks. "Excuse me," I said. "Don't you think that's a bit extreme?"

My mom's glare didn't flicker, and she said, "I'm not kidding, Jodie. Don't walk out that door." A sudden wind whipped passed me, and the candles flared. I could see clearly that her eyes were glistening and I realized she was crying, or about to. My mom is not a crier, so I walked back over to the table. The candle's light danced in the pools of tears surrounding her eyes. She pointed to the chair like a cop and said, "Sit."

Picking up a handful of beans and slowly dropping them into her other hand, she said, "These things take time to change, Jodie, because the mothers and grandmothers need to be convinced to stop it. They can change it, but it's like chipping away at a very hard stone. Their grandmothers' grandmothers had it done. And grandmothers', grandmothers' grandmothers. It's a ritual. It's been going on for generations and could take generations to stop. As for changing the men's minds—forget it.

"When I was helping Pa Sorie count his fish, he told me it's the old women who are the problem, so I asked if he would marry an uncircumcised girl. He snorted and said, 'NO!' so I told him he's part of the problem too."

She rolled her head as if working out a kink in her neck. When she finished three rolls, she looked hard into my eyes. "Jodie, I didn't come only to study women in a fishing village, although that's the main reason. I came to try and start the change process. Discourage circumcision." She laughed at herself. "Plant the seeds to stop it. . . ."

"So everybody agrees with it? And it's going to be this way forever?"

"Everybody," she said. Then she dropped the beans and tapped the tabletop with her finger, punctuating each word as her voiced dropped into a hoarse whisper, "When the women stand together, and a whole age group of girls don't get circumcised, then the men will have to change their minds, for whom will they marry? Women of the world need to unite against it, Jodie, but women where it happens are really the ones who need to stop it. It takes time." She took my hands gently, as if I was little again. "Maybe Khadi's future daughter will be in that first group."

"If she lives. So why aren't you out there talking to them instead of me?"

My mom shook her head slowly and spoke as if she was talking to someone hard of hearing or dense, "What do you think we talk about in the fields everyday—my favorite recipes? Remember how I worked so hard so I could talk about 'it?' That was 'it,' Jodie.

"I bring it up constantly, and now one or two women let me finish my sentence. Before they'd just cut me off, or hoe away from me. Now one or two of them almost listen," she said with a shrug.

"But wait, I thought when we got here you said we weren't here to try to change people. Remember we were going to blend in? Isn't stopping this crazy cutting stuff interfering?"

"Oh, dear. What if you saw a dying baby that you could help. Would you say nothing because you don't want to interfere or get involved?" she asked me.

"But that's what I'm saying," I said, and I heard my voice raise an octave. "I want to get involved. I want to save Khadi!" I stood suddenly and my chair crashed to the floor. Leaning on the table, I said, "Please, Mom, don't say I can't talk to Khadi and warn her. Maybe she'll be the first to decide for herself."

My mom rested her head on her hands, then looked up at me with concern and love and said, "Trying to stop you from talking to Khadi would be like trying to stop a flash flood. You are so much like me. Talk to Khadi about it then, only Khadi. But stay away from the Secret Society, Jodie. Leave the women to me. And if I hear even a whisper about you badgering the women, you'll be in serious trouble like you've never known before. Promise me, Jodie, right now, that you'll only talk to Khadi, and you'll stay far far away from the Sande. It's taboo. Like I said, you're not only not welcome there— you are forbidden.

"The Secret Society is their world, and it's where they draw the line for how far we can enter their world. If we want to stay here, we have to respect that line. So if you can't respect that line, then we'd better go now. It's nothing to mess with, Jodie. Secret Society and juju can make sweet people do strange things."

I flapped my arms like a pelican trying to take off and nearly screamed at my mom, "How can you respect something you totally disagree with?"

"I said I respect their right to draw lines. That's it. There are many good things they do in the Secret Society, it's only that one part I disagree with. I'm not attacking the whole society. We're here to join into life where we are welcome, not invade the little that's held back. Promise me you won't do anything stupid, or get Khadi into trouble. Now."

She was staring at me like a hawk, and I felt like a cornered mouse. *Do I make a promise I know I won't keep?* I asked myself. Instead, I answered her question with a question, in hopes that she'd forget the promise.

It was rotten, but I couldn't resist saying, "I guess for

the first time you aren't going to laugh and say, 'Well Jodie, no condition is permanent,' because Khadi's sure will be."

Slowly and sadly my mom nodded her head, then went to her bed. As she lifted her mosquito net, she said, "Say it, Jodie. Say you promise not to interfere."

She suddenly looked older than I'd seen her look before, and her face was sad and stern. Her anxiety forced a reluctant "I promise" from my mouth, but in my gut I knew I was lying.

I blew out the sputtering candle and we both went to bed feeling rotten.

12

BEFORE THE SUN SHONE ABOVE THE HUTS, I was on my way to Khadi's. Life looked suspended in what was normally a busy place. Ma Luba's worn mortar made from a tree stump stood empty. The pestle, like a guard, stood leaning against a mango tree and chickens pecked peacefully around it looking for rice scraps. Goats, stuck in a makeshift pen of sticks, bleated as I passed by, as if I should set them free. Only one woman appeared out of the growing light, a huge fish draped over her head that kissed her right shoulder with huge lips and patted her left shoulder with its wide, flapping tail.

I sat patiently beneath the little roof Khadi's father had built over their cooking fire. I was glad for the extra time, I needed to think what I could say that would save my friend's life. My wrist ached where my mom had gripped it the night before, and my eyes were gritty. The only thing I knew for sure after my sleepless night was there was no time to lose.

Khadi's eyes popped wide when she saw me sitting there. "Wetin da matta?" she asked me.

"Wi need fo talk jus now," I told her. I grabbed her arm and started walking to the beach. It was strange to walk through the silent village, and that silence wrapped itself around us. At the shore the tide was low, and the water lapped against the sand. We walked without talking until I picked a spot to sit, then I pulled her down with me.

"Yu no fo start," she said to me. "Wi no go talk Sande."

She made me angry, so I yelled, "Yu want fo die?" That was not what I wanted to say.

I could only see the outline of her face in the growing light, but I could feel her anger. It's not how I wanted to start, so I said, "Khadi, sistah pas best, yu want fo die? That's wetin they do in Sande."

"Kill people, yu mean fo say? If dat be so, how is it wi get women in da village? Why all not dead dead already? Dey all dun Sande, and dey no die."

"Du ya, please please, listen fo jus five minutes. Yu no de gree, wi no de talk Sande no mo." I knew it was a lie as I said it, but I needed to warn her and help her escape if she wanted. The first glimmer of the sun rose off my shoulder, and I could see Khadi's face clearly. Her eyes were glaring at me and her face was stonelike. I rushed on, losing my Krio as I went, "Khadi, do you really know what they do to you? Yu sabe, I mean really know what they do? They cut you, in the place where no one should touch you without your permission."

"Who say so?"

"My mother. She talks all de time in the fields against dis ting. Ask any woman, Ah be sure de say my mother talk too much, jus lek me. But she has to. De plenty bad tings go with cutting, Khadi. Yu want infection? Bad bad infection, which make yu sterile?"

She just stared at the beach, refusing to look my way.

When I said, "And no sexual pleasure," her head popped up.

"Wetin dat mean?" she asked.

"Yu sabe. Like yu get a fine time with a man?" I looked away from her widening eyes and watched the small waves rush ashore.

"Yu sabe dis pleasure?" she asked me. Her face was softening a bit, not so angry looking and more like herself.

"Ah no fo sabe direct direct," I told her. "But I've read enough books and seen enough movies to know it looks like fine. It looks like something Ah wan fo try one day." I couldn't believe I'd said that out loud, but it was out there.

Khadi stood and faced the ocean. She put her hands on her hips, and tensed the muscles in her shoulders.

"Ah no fo worry bout pleasure," she said. "But wetin dis mean, sterile?"

"It means no babies. Yu no able fo get pikin. Jus like Auntie Soba."

She twisted around like a tornado and said, "No babies? But Ah no get cut, Ah no get married. Same same: No babies."

"Some no marry and still get pikins," I said, not sure where I was going with it. "Women, Ma Jemma, she no de get man but she get pikin."

"She no de get plenty. No respect. No friends. But plenty palaver. But it be tru, she get pikin."

"Khadi, let's run away," I said, grabbing her hand. "Let wi go, jus now. It could save your life. People die from it."

She looked me in the eye and said, "Now yu go too far. If it kills de be no women at all. How Ah get me mother if it kills?"

"Obviously it doesn't kill everyone, but jus one is too many. And I can't let you take that chance."

A sudden fire lit in her eyes and she said, "Yu go fo tell me wetin Ah need fo do? Yu de one never lissen no side, yu go fo tell me? Ah no able fo believe. Yu de run yu life, Ah de run mine. Wi no go fo talk dis ever again. Yu de talk, wi de finish being friends. Padi no mo."

Then she brushed the sand off her lapa and turned to go. She walked up the beach a bit, her shoulders tight and her back as rigid as a pole. Twisting on one foot, she turned to me and said, "It be up to yu. No mo questions or no mo padis. Now Ah need fo go, the day it be beginning."

I stood on the beach for a long time, watching the waves grow as the tide rose. The men heading out to sea in their tiny dug-out canoes paddled through the building surf. That was two out of two people telling me to stay away. Mind my own business. Let my friend risk death. My mom and Khadi, the two people who meant the most to me in the world. And what about that snake woman I saw in the marketplace, shaking her bag at me?

Should I listen? I asked myself.

"Can I listen?" I said out loud. The answer wasn't in the stretches of white beach that ran away from me in both directions. Or in the waves, that were gently building. They lapped at my feet like warm kisses, so I waded into the surf trying to figure out what to do next. It was strange, but in the warm water I felt cold and as numb as a gum filled with Novocaine.

13

IT SEEMED TO ME THAT THE FIRST STEP WOULD be to quit asking questions. Just back off and pretend that I was relieved to be free of the Secret Society stuff. It was difficult. At sunset each evening singing voices and hand clapping swelled through Bukama. Excitement in the village grew, like a snowball heading downhill. I got so good at ignoring the women that my mom thought my ears were going bad.

It should have been magical with the drums and the dancing, but instead it only added to my bad mood and determination. After three weeks of letting the subject drop, I made my first plan. I'm sure everyone thought I had forgotten about the Society, but like I said, I'm a slow learner. I'm no good at taking advice, no matter how good it might be. Especially if I think I'm right. Taboo or not, I had to see what was going on.

Every Thursday morning, before the first rays of light crept up behind the huts, the girls eleven to fifteen left the village for a secret gathering spot. I just happened to be awake one Thursday, and going to the latrine when I saw which way they left. Hanging back, I followed behind them, all talking and giggling like nervous kids, to the first fork in the trail, then rushed home and got back into bed. The little snuffles coming from behind my mother's mosquito net told me she was sleeping soundly.

I spent a lonely morning getting water at the well, pounding some rice and listening to the silence of the deserted village. A few old men sat in the central bafa, talking in spurts. All the women were either in the fields or with the Secret Society. Life just wasn't the same without Khadi. In the afternoon, I went to look for firewood. It wasn't a coincidence that I followed the path the girls had taken in the dawn light.

I walked slowly, straining for the sound of someone talking or singing, or maybe even screaming. I had no idea what went on at these sessions to learn how to be a woman and wife. At least what went on before the cutting. The path split and I wandered to the left into a forest. My heart beat double time and my hands began to sweat. I stopped for a few deep breaths, telling myself, *You do what you gotta do*. Even if it meant breaking taboo.

A faint path showed through the trees, and I walked on with more reluctance than before. I kept thinking about getting lost or stepping on a snake when I heard the voices. Through the trees I could see the girls returning to the village, walking along singing and waving branches in the air. They were each covered in oil, and their bodies shone like black marble. Each girl had a faraway look on her face as she sang and swayed her branch, marching through the thick forest. Nobody saw me because they were all in another world.

I ducked behind the trunk of a dead cotton tree, then turned and ran back down the path I had entered on. At the fork I took the other path away from the village and started searching for firewood. For someone who had gone collecting over an hour before, I had very little to show for it. I grabbed any loose stick and found a log that someone else must have dropped. It was totally uncool, because she'd probably be back for it, but I took it, putting it on my head, and wandered back toward the village.

The girls and I arrived at the same time. By cutting behind the huts, I came from the opposite direction, laden with wood. They arrived empty handed and happy. Khadi came over and took the log from my head. "Ow di go de go?" she asked.

I took her hand and said, "Fine-o." It was clear she didn't have a clue that I had nearly met them on the forbidden path as they returned from the secret gathering spot.

And I didn't have a clue that I had set some bad luck in motion.

THE NIGHT WAS A QUIET ONE FOR THE VILLAGE. Most of the girls my age were exhausted, so getting water at the well was pretty subdued. People were out, but they were all taking care of business. Just quiet work was underway when the settling stillness was shattered by the shrill shrieks of women, screaming. Everyone jumped to life immediately, running to see what was going on. Any other night the screams would not have been so loud or overwhelming. Any other night radios and shouts of playing kids and wails of tired babies filled the air.

As the screams got louder, suddenly, from behind the mango tree, Joko came charging to the rescue. Running full on, he held a ten-foot snake stick and a flashlight, arm cocked ready for action.

He charged up to the shrieking women and with one resounding thump he killed the snake. Silence followed. Everyone feared snakes, for they had all lost at least one relative to a snakebite. And Joko had saved someone with his quick action. He had looked so graceful as he ran and attacked in one smooth action. *What a guy*, I thought, until he picked up the dead snake on his stick and proceeded to chase the women he'd just saved with it.

The women scattered, shrieking louder than before. Joko turned and saw me watching the whole thing. He wandered over, snake dangling off his stick. I'm no snake fan, but I was sorry to see that it was a young python. It was about four-and a-half feet long, with a fine green-and-black mosaic pattern wrapped around the snake's bulky body.

"Na shame-o," I said. "He no be poisonous, but he sure be dead."

Joko's face lit up as he asked me, "Yu get one bag or basket fo me?"

I gave Joko an old rice sack for the snake.

"Wetin yu do with him? Skin it and sell it?" I asked.

He grinned, like a five year old, "No. Ah de make play. Chase everyone every-which-way."

It was clear that the crowd that had gathered didn't approve, for as a team they all started to suck their teeth. Joko took no notice as he shoved his bag at Khadi's little sister, Fatima. Khadi's father stepped forward, his head, covered with a small white prayer cap, was inches above Joko's.

He didn't say a word, but he glared down at Joko. He tapped his fly whisk against his left palm while Joko bundled up his bag and ran for home. Slowly the crowd drifted to their huts. I was tired too, having been sneaking around since before sunup. One by one, the faint glow of candles and lanterns disappeared from hut windows. A peaceful quiet descended upon the village again, like a welcome blanket.

I DROPPED MY LAPA TO THE FLOOR AND SET my flashlight where I could reach it beside my bed. My mom, making notes about her day gutting a huge catch of fish by the light of the lamp, gave me a wave and said, " 'Night, dear. Sleep tight and don't let the bed bugs bite."

Lying there like a corpse, I suddenly felt something on my leg. I screamed when I saw a giant scorpion, pointed tail twitching above its head, looking for a place to sink its stinger into me. With a sweep of my hand I knocked it off, then nearly ripped my net from the roof trying to get out from under it.

I grabbed a flip-flop and began beating on the scorpion. His reddish-black back shined in the flashlight beam, and he fought fiercely to escape. But I was crazy and smashed him until he was no more than a smear upon the floor. My mom, scattering her notes every which way, jumped from the table and grabbed my flailing arm. "Enough, enough," she said, taking the flip-flop from my hand and hugging me. "It's dead, and you did a good job. Now let's just double-check your bed and mine for any others lingering, then you can go to sleep. You can even have my bed if it makes you feel better."

We tore the sheets off the tick mattresses and shone the flashlight and lantern carefully around the bed and beneath it. We searched up the walls and around the windowsills, and found nothing but an empty carcass of a cockroach long dead.

By the time we had demolished and rearranged the hut I was exhausted. It was like sleep stood off in the far corner of the room, staring at me but not enveloping me. Lying in the dark, listening to my mom's little snuffles, I had a sudden revelation. First the snake that Joko killed, then the scorpion in my bed. Was there any connection between my first intrusion into the Secret Society and my first scorpion and snake?

"In the land of juju," my mother had said one night, "anything is possible. Don't mess with it, Jodie. Juju is taboo, and taboo means hands off. Stories I could tell . . ."

I was sure my mom could tell me if these things were connected to my spying or just coincidence, but I couldn't ask her or anyone else. For if I did I would give myself away—and possibly the life of my best friend.

14

TO MAKE SURE NO ONE KNEW I WAS FOLLOW-
ing the group, I let one week go by, then followed the
girls again. The warnings—if they were warnings—didn't
stop me. I had to know what they were doing all day.
And where they were in case I had to save Khadi. Staying far behind them, but listening to their singing voices,
I followed them to the secret gathering spot. It was my
first time there, and the place gave me the creeps. It was
totally surrounded by tons of firewood in a broken forest. I had asked Khadi about the area months before,
and she said that no one collected wood from that place
because it was dangerous. She refused to say what made
it dangerous. Now I realized that she'd known about the
Secret Society way back then, before she was a member-
in-training. Standing there alone, surrounded by broken
branches with sharp tips and dangling leaves on thin spiders' webs, I understood what she meant about danger-

ous. The energy of the place sent small chills up my back.

Old broken tree limbs pierced the sky, and the forest floor was a scatter of branches and twigs. If it hadn't been for the women beating on tin washtubs I could never have entered the forest—every step sent up a loud crunching chorus. There was no clear path visible, and as I quietly crashed my way through the forest, I realized just how well-chosen the spot was. Only a fool would risk making so much noise in such a natural burglar alarm system.

The drumbeats stopped and I had to freeze. I was surrounded by branches draped with spiders' webs, dusty with age and littered with hollow insect carcasses. It was clear that I was off whatever path they had used, for no one had walked here for ages. Not a dusty spider's web was broken.

When the drumming started up again, I looked behind me. My back ached from hunching down, and there were little red welt lines crisscrossing my arms. I looked for signs of where I'd just passed, but it was impossible to know which branches were newly broken. The drums were beating double time, and the deep throb of them seemed to surround me like the sound in a movie theater.

My feet moved by themselves as my mind caught the drum and beat into my head, "Don't get lost. Don't get caught. Don't get lost . . ." I moved toward the drum-beats, breaking branches and collecting scratches in a hypnotized state. It seemed like hours passed when suddenly I spotted a clearing up ahead.

A small hut stood behind a wide space swept clean, and the forest of broken branches stood close around the clearing, as if protecting it from intruders. Like me. I craned to look around a thick old branch and saw a sight I'll never forget. All the girls were dancing in a large circle, humping to the drumbeats and Ma Jalloh's song. The girls danced without any inhibitions, like drunken puppets shaking on strings.

Ma Luba, a short, stocky woman with a thousand wrinkles across her face, suddenly caught the excitement, and jumped into the center of the circle. She shook her butt as if caught in a wild, uncontrollable spasm, and Ma Jalloh called out, "HEY HEY HEY!" The beat increased until Ma Luba could dance no more. She fell to the ground, sweating and twitching and smiling.

Ma Jalloh sang, and the girls answered back, "Du ya, du ya, du ya," and the drums kept beating. Salimatu held an upturned washbasin for her sister, who beat it with her head back and her eyes tightly closed. I watched, entranced and frightened. I knew I didn't belong there, but the sounds sucked me in. I wanted to leave and I wanted to watch, and over the tug of war my mind kept shouting, "Don't get caught. Don't get lost."

I couldn't help but wonder, as I watched, what was the big deal? They danced and sang every night in the village, so why wander into a dead forest to do more of the same? Suddenly Khadi jumped into the circle. She stared before her with unseeing eyes and spread her arms wide. Her torso shimmied below her outstretched arms, as she bounced frantically on the balls of her feet. Soon Jenisa jumped up directly behind Khadi, so close their arms touched, as they shook from the shoulder to the wrist. She mirrored Khadi's pelvis and feet as if they were one. Girl after girl formed into a tightly woven line behind Khadi, more synchronized than watches. I was so entranced I hadn't noticed that a shadow, as dark as spilled ink, had fallen over me. The sun was beginning to set.

I had promised to meet my mom at the hut before sunset, and there was no telling how long it would take me to find my way out. I was in shade, but a diffused sunlight still lit the area behind me. I had to get back.

The pace of the music was speeding up, and I found myself moving madly through the branches, driven by the sound, when the drums stopped suddenly. My bush bashing echoed loudly through the stumps and trunks. I dropped to the ground, making a final crash noise.

Petrified, I lay waiting for the drumming to start. Nothing happened for the longest time. I lay with my nose pressed into a dead leaf pile. Ants were walking freely across my arms and face, and sweat trickling down my forehead stung my eyes. And still the music did not start.

I was lying with teeth clenched, itchy but unable to scratch, scared but unable to cry out for help, when she came into sight. Ma Lidia is the oldest woman in the village. Some say she is one hundred, and others insist she's older. Her eyes were weak, and her hearing bad, but she still moved about like a young woman. Humming softly to herself, she strolled toward the village, along a path that was still invisible to me. If the music started up again, I could follow behind her at a safe distance, and get home before sunset. Without the cover of the drums I could go nowhere.

She passed close enough to see me if she had good eyes. A lapa was tied around her head, and she walked without looking left or right. I stopped breathing. I could feel a stone pressing against my forehead. Inches from my nose a large cockroach cocked his antennae my way. Slowly, he climbed on my hand and I learned what Felix would have called, "the meaning of ultimate self control." I wanted to shout when, sweating buckets and on the verge of screaming, the drums started suddenly. I didn't stop a second, the cockroach went flying one direction and I the other. I found the trail Ma Lidia had taken, but had to control myself not to run too fast and overtake her.

My heart beat faster than any drumbeat I'd ever heard, and as loudly as most. My breathing had turned to little hiccups, and I felt totally out of control. When the wicked forest finally started to thin and it was easier to run, I changed direction and ran toward the sound of the surf. The crash of hard-breaking waves made the memory of the breaking twigs and branches seem ridiculous.

I ran down to the surf line and collapsed on my knees. My lapa was a mess, streaked with dirt and a large tear. I took it off and washed it. The saltwater stung the mosaic of welts on my arms and legs. I submerged myself and stayed there until my lungs nearly burst.

I shot to the surface and was happy to find blue skies, white sand, and no trees or branches. When I felt my heartbeat return to normal I went and laid on the beach. I said to the pelicans flying by, "I will never go back there. Never. I'm sorry Khadi, but I can't. Taboo is strong stuff, and breaking a taboo too scary. Forgive me padi, du ya, Ah beg."

When I got back to the village wet from my swim, I looked like someone on vacation, rather than someone scared half to death. I strolled to our hut and noticed that my mom wasn't there. I changed into a dry lapa and tank top. The sea had taken the red out of my welts, but I smeared them with cream just to be sure. By the time Khadi returned to the village—it was nearly twilight—I was looking like a well-rested lounge lizard compared to her. She glowed.

I watched Khadi for a few days to see if she knew I had followed the group. I tried to get her to go collect wood with me in the direction they had taken, and we did walk for a ways down the path, but then she refused to go any farther saying, "No Jodie. . . ."

In the days that followed, Khadi and her initiation group were gone from the village for longer and longer periods. Though I still saw Khadi at night, I missed her terribly. We had spent months in the fields together, hoeing and weeding and watering. Now during the day I did most things alone, obsessed with how I could save my friend without scaring myself to death, and how to endure such sudden loneliness. Fortunately, the loneliness didn't last long.

chapter

15

IT HAPPENED THREE DAYS IN A ROW. NO MAT-
ter where I was, Khadi's cousin, the snake-killing Joko,
turned up. The first day I was winnowing the hulled rice
in front of the hut. With a rhythmic beat Khadi had
showed me, I tossed the rice from a flat basket into the
air and watched the wind carry away the hulls like flee-
ing moths. One minute I was alone, and the next he was
leaning against a pole on the kitchen we share with Ma
Luba. When I caught sight of him, I nearly tossed the
basket instead of the rice, then demanded, "Why you
want fo scare me like so?"

Joko laughed, then bent to touch his toes, stretching
like a sleek, jet-black Siamese cat. Bent in half, he tilted
his head sideways and up to look at me and said, "Who
be Felix?"

I nearly fainted, and said, "Na who be axsin?" Khadi
must have told him.

"Ah de ax," he said with a solemn face. "It be me."

Stretching up to his full height, he stood a foot taller than me.

Squinting up at him, I asked, "Why?"

Without the slightest pause, he said, "Poo-mui girls get two bo? You know, padi pas padi, friend pas friend?"

"Say what? Dis poo-mui girl gets no bo, no boyfriend. Zero. Zilch. Nada. None!"

"Na lie," he said, pointing over my head into the far distance, "You de get one America side, Felix, and one Bukama side, Joko."

"Chance no de! Ah able fo say Ah no want boyfriend, here or there," I told him, unable to take my eyes off his dark handsome face.

"Wi go see," he said, then turned on his bare heel and sauntered away.

I caught myself smiling as I watched him cruise off. He walked just like he stretched, like a slinky Siamese cat.

That night, as we washed our dishes, my mom casually said, "So how's Joko?"

The tin cup I was drying dropped to the floor with a loud clatter. "Fine I guess. How should I know?"

"Jodie, Bukama is small. When Ma Luba belches in her hut, Pa Sorie hears it in his boat out at sea. What makes you so nervous? It was just a simple question."

"I don't know. Maybe because the way you said it sounded as if I was trying to hide something."

"And are you?" she said, putting our saucepan down carefully into the wooden rack. "Trying to hide something?"

Shaking my head slowly, I said, "No. But what's the big deal? We were right here in front of the hut. And all we did was talk a bit, then he left. Please don't tell me that he's off limits too. He may be the only friend close to my age I have these days."

"Well dear, just let me tell you this one time. This isn't America, and Joko is not Felix. Back home you guys can hang wherever you want, and nobody notices. But here, word travels fast. Young men and women do not meet alone."

Wrapping the dishtowel tightly around my fist I said, "I just don't get it. Here they drag girls off into the bush to teach them about how to treat a man, and yet girls and boys can't talk like two human beings?" I snapped the towel the way we did at swim practice. "And it really bugs me that a place with a big Secret Society that survives on secrets talks about everyone's private lives. We aren't doing anything that needs to be kept secret, but I don't want everyone talking about me. We've only met once, and in a very public place."

"Just make sure it stays that way. And if you have to meet, make it someplace crowded, so folks don't think you're sneaking." She ran her left hand down her right arm, scrapping off the soapsuds that had climbed up her arm. "Do you like him?"

"Come on, Mom. I'm lonely, and Joko is funny. He makes me laugh. I can't predict where we'll meet, but I'm sure we will. Where's all this trust you always talk about?"

"I'm just trying to save you some grief. People talk, stories grow, rumors fly. I trust you, but when you do something out of the ordinary others may not trust you.

"And since we're having this talk, I just want to be sure you're minding your own business. No Secret Society stuff, Jodie." Her face was stern in the lantern light, taking on the steely look whenever we got onto the subject of "it." "You almost scare me—you're being too good. But you've promised and so I believe you. . . ."

I tried to forget my mom's words the next day, especially about trust, while collecting wood out by the lagoon near the beach. Without looking, I watched for Joko. I never had time for him when Khadi was around, but now I had nothing but time. I thought about my mom's talk from the night before. We had only met once without Khadi, and people were already talking. It made me angry. Grumbling as I collected seven long broken branches, I said to myself, "I'll see who I want, when I want." With long swings of the flashing panga I cut the branches into easy-to-carry pieces, mumbling, "Sex! Why do adults always think everything has to do with sex?" Piling my cut wood, it occurred to me that I was stalling a bit, and I finally admitted to myself that I wanted to see Joko again. And as unbelievable as it is, just as I was winding my extra lapa into a head cushion, he appeared.

"Ow di go de go?" he asked.

"Ah tell God tank ya, Ah be fine-o."

We stood there, smiling at one another, when a shrieking hornbill startled us. Joko picked up my neatly stacked pile of wood and put it on my head. Balancing it, I said, "In America the men carry the heavy loads and the women walk along and help if they want."

Snorting like a bull, he said, "Ah feel bad-o fo yu man Felix. Na myself, Ah never do de woman's work. If somebody see such foolishness dey de laugh and laugh. And soon, Joko be done done with all his padi. Dey go fo laugh too much."

We walked along, single file. I had waited on the trail so I could walk behind him and watch him. His long slender build moved as if he was underwater, fluid. He surprised me when he turned back to me and said, "Be happy. Yu de look sad pas words."

"Ah say, is it possible fo a boy and a girl to be padi, no sex, no serious business? Jus be friends? Wetin yu de tink about so?"

"Jodie Jodie," he said. "Wetin get inside your head? Wi

be padi now, maybe more later. But jus now, wi be jus padi."

He leaned down, I'm sure to kiss me, but I arched back and said, "Wait small! We need fo talk."

Joko threw his head back and laughed. "Eh, yu de look scared. Wi go talk and talk tamara. Bout weather, bout chickens, bout whatever yu want. Jus now, Ah de go," and he stepped off the path, whistling as he left.

I figured out what places had the least traffic at what time of day, and then went there in hopes that Joko would come. Once again, doing exactly what my mom said not to do. On the third day I picked the well, at midday, when the sun was highest and few people leave the shade of the bafa or their huts. I had specific questions to ask—questions my mom said not to ask anyone but her. But as Khadi spent more and more time away doing her Secret Society stuff, I felt like I'd never be able to save her. Time was running out. Maybe Joko could tell me some things.

Singing the alphabet under my breath, I pulled the rope up hand over hand. Suddenly, a deep voice joined me, on the PQ—RS version created by Khadi. Actually the alphabet by Khadi was a very popular tune in the work places of the village. Each work spot had it's own rhythm, depending on the job. Mortar and pestle called for a rigid beat to keep the *thunk thunk* going. Washing women sang, as they always did, ABC, DEF, GHI, LMNO, and pulling water from the well called for PQ-RS-TUVW. As I pulled and sang, Joko's strong voice drowned mine out.

"Ow di day?" I asked.

"Tank God, it be fine-o. Ow di bodi?" he replied.

I wanted to say, "What do you think?" but instead settled for, "Ah be well."

The heavy, wet rope in my hands began to slip, and Joko grabbed on to it. "You here fo help wi?" I asked him.

"Sure, Ah de pull, but Ah no de carry." The muscles on his shoulders rippled under a pattern of long, thick scars that shined on their own and ran down his back. Initiation scars. He was a man although he was only sixteen, and one day soon, at fourteen, Khadi would be a woman. She would definitely suffer more getting there.

"Yu be lucky," I said.

He stopped pulling on his rope, and staring straight into my eyes, asked, "Why? Cuz we be friends pas friends?"

"Because you don't have scars like the women. Boys no de suffer to be men like girls do to be women. Once again, the men get it easy," I said, with a frustration that surprised me.

Holding his hand up like a policeman stopping traffic he said, "Yu no fo start. Ah no de talk Sande. Yu go bring me big big trouble yu de talk Secret Society. Wi all know yu get questions yu no need to ask. Man no sabe wetin dey do."

He was literally backing away from me, so I quickly changed the subject. "Wetin yu mean friends pas friends? Listen ow yu de talk."

He looked at me with wide eyes and said, "Not-a-so? Wi de talk and wi de laugh. Yu be fine fine, and Ah be handsome. Na Ah help yu small small."

A sudden warmth ran through my body, something I'd never felt before. He was right, he was very handsome. I looked at his eyes, as black and glistening as the water at the bottom of a well—reflecting the sunlight. A smile, crooked I'm sure, spread across my face and a chill ran through me as he lightly rubbed my arm, shoulder to elbow, up and down.

He shocked me by picking up my bucket and walking away.

"Wetin yu do?" I asked, amazed.

"Ah need fo help me padi pas padi," he replied.

"Now who said wi be padi pas padi?" I could have sounded stronger, but he was carrying my water for me, and it felt good.

We walked along in silence. A slight breeze ruffled the long fronds of the palm trees, and two turtledoves called back and forth, "Work Harder. Work Harderrr." The hoots and calls of three guys that came around a hut up ahead destroyed the silence and pleasure of the moment.

"Na wetin Ah see?" said Jerk Number One.

"Wi live to learn! Ah no de believe!" joined in Jerk Number Two.

"Dis no de gree with the Joko I know!" added Jerk Number Three.

Joko set the bucket down and turned to the guys, "Wi de talk later." Then he turned to me, took my hand for a second and said, "Yu de tink upon us, wi be friends pas friends, or jus padi and padi. Yu able fo say so tamara. Pick another good place wi go meet. Ah de find yu."

AS I LAY IN BED THAT NIGHT I THOUGHT OF Joko, and his smile and how he helped me fill my lonely days. Then I thought about the next day, and where to meet. There was no doubt in my mind where that should be. The washing rock was always empty at midday. Although the work was cool, the walk was long and hot, so most women and girls did the laundry early in the morning.

I washed with an enthusiasm I didn't recognize in myself, picking the lapas up and holding them high, then dropping them down with a splash, and rubbing rubbing rubbing. The sun was hot against my back, a nice contrast to my cool, wet front. An African fish eagle flew overhead, throwing her head back and releasing a call of pure joy. I threw my head back and tried to answer her, then jumped when I heard the whistling. I don't know how long he'd been watching me, but I was embarrassed at my sick birdcall. Squatting on a rock across the river, his daddy longlegs folded beneath him and his arms resting on his knees, was Joko.

His round head was covered with a torn straw hat, set at a cocky angle. Big dimples, even across a river, cast deep shadows on his cheeks. He waved and said, "Eh girl, no need fo work so hard. Wi all get dirty clothes, den get clean, den dirty again. Smile up!" And he did, a mouth of dazzling piano keys surrounded sharply by his full lips.

Standing in one long fluid motion, feet perfectly balanced on a round flat stone the size of a Frisbee, he started toward me. His slender muscular legs looked sculpted, and his long feet and toes seemed to grip slippery stones as he made his way across the river. The water deepened in the middle, climbing up to lick the bottoms of his cutoff jeans. His skin glistened like wet ebony in the sunlight.

I tried not to watch him too closely, but he insisted on talking as he crossed, asking, "Na why fo yu work so hard? Yu get lapas or yu get rags there?"

I leaned back from the pummeled laundry and said, "You go fo show me, bo, you sabe so much."

He leaned over the washing stone and I looked

closely at the scars on the side of his head. Little fanlike lines, spreading outward, sprouted from the corner of each of his eyes. I jerked back, for I knew they were more initiation scars. Before I thought I blurted out, "You're part of the problem."

He stood straight, placing his soapy hands on his skinny hips, and said, "Ah give no palaver, Ah take no palaver, and Ah live no palaver. Yu de get problem, dat be yu problem. Yu own palaver.

"Anyways, a rich poo-mui girl cannot suffer too too much. To be a man is not easy."

I laughed out loud. "Ah de see the same same poda-poda," I told him. Then with a snort I said, "Try being a woman."

"Yu no be woman," he told me. "Yu de be pikin still."

"Hardly," I said. "I de be fifteen in no time."

I didn't realize I had stuck my chin out until he took it in his fingertips. He cocked my head to one side and said, "Yu de get eyes pas beau-tiiii-ful. Silver, jus like the blade of a fine fine new panga."

I gazed back at him uncertain what to do. He smiled sweetly then bent to kiss me. With a dazed dip to the right, I stopped him by squealing, "Na wetin you mean, rich poo-mui girl? Ah no de be rich."

"To God," he said with a puff of breath. "Wi all sabe dat every every poo-mui be rich. Yu get plenty cars, plenty ice, plenty cows and plenty plenty."

"Is that why yu want fo be my boyfriend? Because Ah be rich, or because Ah be poo-mui?"

"Mercy no de," he said sadly shaking his head. "Ah no be able fo hear dis talk-o." He rinsed his hands off and said, "Wi go see."

I didn't want him to leave, especially hurt, so I said, "Wait small." He was looming over me, my head just reaching his shoulder. Carefully standing on my tiptoes I stretched up and kissed him. I felt the smoothness of his full mouth, and the softness of his lips.

Quickly I snatched up my pile of laundry and climbed the bank. Turning back, I said, "Wi go see." There he stood, as still as a heron looking for fish, in the water by the washing rock. His smile, spreading from dimple to dimple, sent another flash of warmth and excitement through my body. Suddenly I was scared. One minute I was trying to save Khadi and the next I was kissing her cousin.

"Du ya, Ah beg," I said all flustered. "Dat no be de plan. Ah no want fo make complications wit yu. Ah only want fo save Khadi. Ah beg, I'm sorry."

Putting my laundry pan on my head, I said, "Let me go, before wi make our own Secret Society." For a second I had the crazy thought of checking out sexual pleasure so I could tell Khadi if it were true what people say and the movies show. Maybe that would be enough to make her want to save herself. But no sooner had the thought arrived than a shiver of fear ran down my spine. My mom had once said, while watching two young prostitutes on a street corner in San Diego, "Desperate women seek desperate solutions."

Shaking my shoulders to get rid of the whole scary notion, I said out loud, "I'm not that desperate—yet."

"Say what?" Joko called out from the river.

My headpan of laundry slid sideways as I jerked around. I had completely forgotten he was still there. "Confusion de," I said to him as I shifted my pan back into the right position and quickly left.

16

ON ONE OF HER RARE OFF DAYS FROM SANDE business, Khadi and I went to the beach. The waves were rolling gently in from South America as we sat on the hard wet sand. Khadi had a small, sharp piece of seashell and wrote in strong letters in the sand JODIE. I smiled widely and asked, "Now when yu gettin so smart? Ow yu sabe ow fo spell my nem?"

Smiling with pride, she said, "Ah de read yu envelope from Felix. He be yu bo?"

I squinted a look at her, and said, "No. Ah no get bo. Why fo yu ask me?"

Drawing the alphabet in the sand, she said, "Ah de hear yu get one bo here." Then with flair she wrote in large letters JOKO.

I grabbed her writing hand and said, "Ah no get bo. Ah get padi." Then still holding her hand I guided her to write = PADI across from JOKO.

"Joko equals padi," I said, underlining each word

and sign in the sand as I said it. "Yu get a bo?" I asked her.

"No. Ah no want bo jus now," she said as she stood. Holding her lapa up, she wandered into the surf until the waves washed her calves. Changing the subject without changing her position, she asked, "Ah want one one ting now. Yu know ow fo swim?"

"Ta God, Ah do. Yu want fo lan?" I asked, jumping to my feet and running into the water. Khadi, like most villagers, would wade into the water when it was calm, but never swim. Before she could change her mind, I said, "Step one is take off this lapa." I waved the wet cloth around my head like a looney, screaming "Free! Free at last!"

"Yu done lost yu sense again?" she asked, laughing. "Yu able fo teach swimmin lek yu teach reading na writing?"

"You bet your booties," I said.

"Ah no sabe dis talk. Yu able or no?"

Taking her hand, I said, "Furst yu need fo drop de lapa. Then wi go do back float. But yu need fo trust me, yu able fo do so?" I felt a little guilty asking her that, for even if I hadn't followed her group recently, I had twice. So I was no better than a spy—asking for trust. Huh.

Without a moment's hesitation she took off her lapa, waved it around her head like a looney, then said, "Wetin de next step?"

We spent hours in the warm sea. I held her chin back

and held her back up, all the while talking softly about the beautiful blue skies and warm water to relax her. Slowly I let go of her chin, and she smiled with her eyes closed, keeping her chin pointed at the sky. It took her a moment to realize that I had removed my hand from her back, and when I did she jackknifed into a sitting position and sank.

"Yu no sabe, but yu de float a long time by yu own self."

"Na tru? Yu able fo help me start again? Ah go try once more."

When she was settled again, I removed my hand from her back. This time she felt me move and smiled wide, chin up, floating like a champ. "Wi be lucky pas words," I said. "Now wi get two places to relax, the magic stone and floating in de sea."

"Na tru. Wi be lucky, pas words, but Ah be bad luck too bad ifn Ah don't get to work soon. Yu want fo help wi?" she asked me.

As we waded out of the water I noticed how my T-shirt hugged my blooming body. I looked at my breasts wrapped in the wet cloth, and thought, *I'm almost a woman.* I took my lapa and wound it around myself so I could hug my new body. Khadi watched me twirl, then joined in. Like slow-motion tops, two beautiful young women, black and white, danced side by side on the beach. Grabbing my arms, Khadi said, "Let wi go work."

I thought the work was pretty easy until Khadi started with the questions. Out of the clear blue she asked, "Where is yu father?"

We were shelling peanuts under the mango tree, and I looked surprised when she asked. We'd been best friends for five months, and she had never asked. My look must have said something, for she said, "Why only yu get fo ask questions?"

"My dad is in California. He and my mom got divorced when I was nine. He's married again," I said as casually as I could, but feeling an old anger rise. My father and I didn't talk in the States, and definitely didn't write from Africa.

"Fo why he divorce Sistah Val?" she asked.

"What makes you think he divorced her?"

"A woman able fo divorce a man?" she asked seriously.

"Of course. Can't you here?"

"It is very very rare. Na wetin he dun?" she asked with a thoughtful look on her face.

"Like he got another girlfriend."

"So? Most men here get plenty wifes. Did your mother not want a co-wife?"

I had to laugh out loud. My mom, Sistah Val, the co-wife. Never. Khadi was still very serious, so I explained, "In the U.S. people don't have multiple wives, because the women no de gree. De no allow it. I be sure there are other reasons too, but that is a main one."

Khadi picked up a giant leaf that had just fallen into her lap, "A woman should always obey her husband."

I choked and said, "No way! I barely obey my mom so why would I ever obey a husband? Women and men are equal."

She surprised me by agreeing, sort of, when she said, "Women are as strong as men. Wi de carry plenty water and firewood and working in de fields."

"I don't mean just physically. Women be as smart as men. I've always known that. My mom told me years ago. Women have as much right as any man to work where they want, or study, or get married or not."

She shifted as a ray of sunlight broke through branches of the mango tree and pierced her eyes. "But yu must get married. Na get pikin."

"Ah only able fo say is that I'd rather live alone than have someone try to tell me what to do." I threw the handful of groundnuts so hard into the headpan that they skidded up and out the other side.

Khadi shot me a horrified look and said quickly, "Bad man bete pas emti os."

I made her repeat it and said, "A bad man is better than an empty house?"

She smiled and nodded her head yes.

"Do you really think that it's better to be with a bad husband than be alone?"

"Not-a-so?" she asked without hesitation.

"Is this what the Secret Society teaches you?" I asked with more anger than I meant to.

She looked me in the eye, "No fo start again, mi padi. Wi no fo talk Sande, not now—not never."

Her jaw set so rigidly that I could see the muscles twitching beneath her skin. It was the direct opposite of her relaxed jaw while back floating only an hour before. The day had been so great I didn't want to spoil any of it, so I backed off to keep the peace. We worked silently, breaking the peanut shells, then rubbing the paper-thin skin off. Kids ran around us, screaming with delight as a dog chased them.

I watched an old, bent man set up his barbershop next to us. The shade of the mango tree spread across the ground like a spill. He laid out a burlap bag and placed upon it his scissors, comb, dull razor and mirror. Placing a wooden stool behind the bag, he squatted down to await business.

The barber started tapping on the leg of his stool, sending out a steady beat to attract customers. Joko was the first to arrive. I hadn't seen him since the kiss by the river the day before. We smiled at one another, and Khadi cocked her head like a dog catching a sniff of something. "Joko de," he announced, then sat on the stool and picked up the mirror. Gazing at himself he said, "Ah be too too fine-o. Yu be fine-o too," he said as he handed it to me. "Get a look."

I looked at my face. Sky blue eyes, dark eyebrows and long blond hair that kids love to yank to see if it is real. From my days in the fields and at the river my skin had darkened to a deep rich brown. The tan helped, but still it was not a remarkable face—nothing to write home about. Just a face.

Then I passed the mirror to Khadi. She looked shyly at her reflection, which showed wide, bright eyes, sharp cheekbones, and a smile of straight white teeth. Her black skin, the color of chocolate in the bottom of a cup, was smooth and shiny. She definitely had a face worth writing home about.

We looked at each other closely in the small mirror, then she surprised me by saying, "Yu be too beautiful pas words."

I was shocked. And embarrassed. And very pleased. "Tank ya," I said, "but yu are the one beautiful pas words."

Her hair was braided in one tight line that started on her neck and slowly wound its way around her skull. Tight concentric circles ended at the top of her head in a little palm tree.

I followed the line around her head with my finger-tip, flicking the palm tree on top. We both laughed, then hugged. It was the closest we'd been since the Secret Society business began.

* * *

THE SNIP-SNIP OF THE BARBER'S SCISSORS filled the air. I passed the mirror back to Joko so he could watch the flying hands of the barber work their way around his head. Like everything else in Sierra Leone, the barber worked to a rhythm. He'd snip four times, then bang his scissors against the comb in his other hand. Snip-snip-snip-snip-clunk. His hands worked at lightning speed around Joko's head.

When he finished, the barber rested a hand on each of Joko's shoulders, palms up. Joko dug into the pockets of his baggy pants, then placed a big ripe Guinea mango in each of the barber's hands on his shoulders. The barber sat the mangoes on the cloth displaying his tools, then removed the cloth from Joko's shoulders. Joko took a little scrap of newspaper from his huge pockets and wrapped his hair clippings in it. He held it up and said, "Now nobody able fo do juju against me." He stuffed it into his pocket. Khadi's eyes were glued to the mangoes as she jumped up and grabbed our clean peanuts. "Ah need for fix de chop just now."

Joko sat beside me and said, "Yu de look happy."

"Ah be happy. Ah get one whole day wit my best best friend. Ah be gladdie." I stood to leave and Joko jumped up too, asking, "Which side yu go jus now?"

"Wi go see later," I told him.

I strolled toward our hut, intent on enjoying the

mood. A whole day with Khadi was a rare treat. And a quick meeting with Joko, all at the same time. I could feel the smile on my face, and felt so relaxed that I was totally unprepared for what happened next.

IT WAS DARK AND COOL IN THE HUT. AS I moved away from the doorway and some light fell into the room something caught my eye. In less time than it takes to sneeze I was looking eye to eye with a black spitting cobra.

He stood up like a snake in a charmer's basket. His beady eyes glared at me and his hooded neck flared, stretching two red lines across his broadened neck. He tilted his head back and opened his mouth wide. His fangs shone dully in the light.

I dove through the door to avoid the poison spit coming. My hands scraped along the rough ground, and I crashed my shoulder into a half-buried rock as I rolled away in desperation.

My screams reached far and wide. Villagers came running toward me from all directions. Pa Sorie reached me first and helped me up. "Wetin de happen?" he shouted in my face.

All I could do was shake from head to toe and screech, "Snake. Big big snake!"

Snakes are second nature in Sierra Leone. One man grabbed some dried thatch from the roof, while Ma Judy brought a burning stick from her cooking fire. Salimatu ran to her hut for water. The thatch was piled just inside the doorway of our hut. Pa Sorie lit it with the burning stick, then fanned the flames.

"Wetin yu do?" I screamed. "Yu no need fo burn da hut." I wanted to run over and grab his flaming stick, but I couldn't move. Especially towards the hut.

As soon as the thatch cracked with the growing flames, he threw the gourd of water on it. A billowing cloud of smoke rose up, and Pa Sorie fanned it with a lapa, sending all the smoke inside. I then noticed the men standing at the two windows on either side of the hut. One had a heavy stick and the other a sharp metal panga. It didn't take long for the snake, groggy from the smoke but still very angry, to appear at a window.

His head poked out, and with one swift motion, Jalloh whacked it off with his panga. We heard a thump as its body hit the floor inside the hut. Everyone was talking at once as they examined the large head on the ground.

With a torch in one hand and a long panga in the other, Pa Sorie stepped inside the hut. He looked beneath our wooden beds and behind our cupboard. He played his torchlight around the thatch roof. Satisfied that there were no more snakes, he lifted the carcass on the end of his blade and brought it outside.

He dropped the body near me. It was as thick as my wrist, and at least six feet long. It's dull skin absorbed the light, and sent another run of shakes through my body.

Pa Sorie said, "Ah want fo show yu sometin." He took my arm and led me toward the hut, but I resisted. He said, "Jus come look. Ah need fo show you jus one ting."

Slowly I followed him to the doorway. He shined his light on the wall next to my head. It was where I had been standing when I met the snake. Running down it, like two trails of tears, was the cobra's venom. The stains started even with my eyes, and slowly dripped down the hardened mud wall.

"If yu no able fo move like gazelle, yu de be blind jus now," he said. There was brightness in his eyes, like pride or maybe amazement. He turned me back toward the sunlight and said, "Yu need fo sidom lili bit, na rest."

From nowhere Khadi took my hand and led me to the beach. I needed the space and the light, so we sat on the wide white sand, just touching fingertips.

Once I felt I could control the quiver in my voice I told my friend, "There's no way I'm sleeping in that hut again."

She stroked my fingers and told two passing boys something I couldn't understand. They raced back to the village.

We didn't talk. Her silence gave me strength, and slowly I calmed down. After about an hour she said, "Le wi go fix chop."

When we walked into the village, I saw where the boys had gone. A group had moved our beds out to the mango tree not too far from our hut. They were just hanging our mosquito nets when my mother came running across the compound.

She rushed up to me with looks of terror and relief shifting double time across her face. Word travels very fast in a village with no phones.

"Oh, honey," she said, and took me into her arms. I knew there were people watching, but it had all been too much, so I didn't resist. I released a flood of tears that had been blocked by the shock.

Khadi came up to me and hugged me from behind. My mom's hug stretched around Khadi, and the three of us stood connected. Slowly, some of the fear flowed out and some peace came in.

That night, in the muffled glow of moonlight through mango leaves, I couldn't sleep. Suddenly, I could see the snake's eyes looking directly into mine. I sat up with a jerk and realized I'd seen those eyes before, on the old snake woman in the market.

That gave me someone else to blame for the new bad luck that was following me. It was easier than admitting that snakes and scorpions had entered my life after I had started my spying. If I had figured that out, we'd probably still be there.

17

MY PLEDGE ON THE BEACH NEVER TO RETURN
to the secret spot lasted five days. Khadi and I were
pounding rice one night after dinner in the weak light of
a quarter moon. We were a good team, never missing a
thunk just like those women I had watched in Freetown
that first morning. Khadi sang the alphabet, "AB-CDE-
F-GH," to an African beat as we worked together.

Suddenly Khadi ruined our rhythm when she said,
"Ah go lef yu tamara."

"What do you mean you're leaving me tamara? Like
wi dun finish dis friendship?" I asked, trying to make a
joke.

"Wi no meks pan fomful," she said with a serious
look.

"I don't understand," I said.

"Ah say, wi talk serious business. Wi no fo ful around
jus now. My age group, we go leave tamara fo sometime."

"Yu de go tamara? For sometime! Wetin sometime mean? A month? A year? A week?" I asked. Anger and fear were creeping into my voice, so I stopped talking.

She shrugged her shoulders and said, "Ah no able fo say. One month, five weeks." Then her eyes lit up as if someone had opened a window in them and she said, "Ah de be a woman when ah reech back."

"Yu mean yu want fo maybe die? Yu go take this big chance?" I whined.

Her shining eyes got steely black and she shook her head as she said, "Yu tu trangga too much."

I stuck out my chin and said, "I'm not stubborn. Well, not too stubborn." I put down my pestle and looked into her shining black eyes. "Oh, Khadi, let wi tu go together, escape, jus now."

Khadi froze with her pounding stick hanging in the air. She looked at me with her mouth hanging open. Then she said, "Ah no lie—yu mek me speechless. No. No. No. Yu no lan sens yet? Yu no able fo go, and Ah no wan fo escape."

She said "escape" like someone with a terrible taste in her mouth and it suddenly dawned on me that she wanted to do this Sande stuff.

"So wat oclock yu do go?" I asked, backing off a bit.

"Ah say, wen de sun no komot yet."

"You could die!"

"Jodie, no de humbug me, du ya, Ah beg. Wi no able fo talk, so wi go see." With that she took the rice we had just pounded and stomped off.

"I'll save you," I shouted, but she didn't turn back. She just swung her arm in the air like someone chasing away a pesky fly.

I could see small changes in Khadi just from disappearing once a week for the day. It was almost as if she was getting like Lisa, something I never thought could happen. One day, a few weeks before, we were grinding peanuts to make a paste for groundnut stew, when she suddenly said, "Wen I get pikin wi go eat fish and groundnut every every day."

"Wen yu get pikin? Yu du plan dis time fo dat time?" I asked. I couldn't believe it. At fourteen! She was as bad as Lisa. Didn't anyone my age want to have fun? Be a kid for as long as possible? Then I suddenly realized that I hadn't thought of America or Lisa or even Felix for weeks. My life was so full and busy that I didn't miss anyone or anything. I was here now, with my best friend, living a life I could never have imagined.

What would a month or five weeks do to Khadi? Would I even know my best friend anymore? And would she even want a best poo-mui friend when she came back? In my gut I knew something was out to destroy our friendship, and maybe her life.

I don't think so, I nearly said out loud. *Don't lose her. Do whatever you have to. Save her, even if she doesn't want it now. She'll thank you later.*

Confused, for time had run out for convincing Khadi, I ran down the path to Joko's compound. I needed someone to talk to, and not my mom. Joko was the only other person I could think of.

"Saful saful," I said to myself out loud. "Go slowly, and tink."

I PLOPPED DOWN ON A ROCK BESIDE THE path, wishing I wasn't too scared to go to the "Ah de craze" rock by myself at night. But that was not an option. I sat and thought. Khadi was the best friend I'd ever had. She could read my thoughts, foreign at that, faster than my mom. I thought back to the early days, when I had diarrhea that nearly tore my guts apart. Trips to the latrine were frequent, and always, when I came out, Khadi stood by with a wet cloth for my red, unhappy face.

On the third day, when my stomach was settling and the cramps were calming down, I had asked Khadi, "Do you know how many friends I have back home who would follow me to the toilet? For days? None. Not-a-one."

I had taken her hand and she smoothed the fair hairs

on my arm. She was touched, I could tell, because she spoke without looking up. "If you go fodom fo me, Ah go fodom fo you. Yu be jus like so too."

It took a while, but I finally got it. "If you fall down for me, I fall down for you? Is that it? You help me and I help you?" She had smiled and shook her head yes.

Suddenly, perched on my rock in the thick darkness, surrounded by the deep bellow of frogs in the rice fields and the buzz of mosquitoes, I felt as if she was standing behind me, nodding again, and I knew that it was my turn to go fodom for her. "But how?" I asked the croaking frogs.

There was a still lot of activity as I wandered through the village looking for Joko. He wasn't with the guys playing dominoes on Pa Sorie's porch. Or sitting in the bafa listening to Pa Sisay, the official village historian, talk talk talk. I ran to his favorite little bar, and there he sat on the railing with one leg on each side, like Roy Rogers on Trigger.

"Wi need fo talk," I said.

His friends, the same jerks who had laughed at him for carrying my water, were sneaking looks at one another and trying to hide smiles. Joko looked at them all and said, "Wi go see. Some of us be lucky pas words, and others luck no de. Wi know who de get luck, not-a-so?"

Taking my arm, he walked with me to the edge of the beach, where my mom and I had watched the woman dancing by the grill one evening. Joko tried to sit, but I said, "No. Wi need fo go dark dark," and I dragged him along. I didn't know exactly what I meant or what I wanted, and yet maybe I did know. My heart was beating just as if I'd run a mile. Maybe I wanted to find out what it was like so I could tell Khadi. Maybe that was the only thing left to convince her.

"Jodie, du ya, Ah beg, wetin Ah go do fo una? Yu de act crazed like."

"Please come, just a bit farther. Maybe, just maybe, wi need for have sex, jus now."

He dug his heels into the sand, and threw his head back and laughed. "Ah beg padin," he said, when his hoots calmed down.

Without a word he bent down and kissed me, like I'd never been kissed before. His right hand held the back of my head in a tender cup, and his other hand stroked my back, while his tongue quietly snuck into my mouth. I closed my eyes, scared and happy and confused.

"Wait small," he said, as he let go of me and walked over to a nearby coconut tree. A hammock was wrapped around its base, and quickly Joko untied it and laid it on the ground. "Yu need for lie down," he said.

"No no no. Wi need fo talk first."

"Ah de gree. One minute you no be sure if wi be friends pas friends, na da next minute you want fo make sex. Ah no able for understand, but Ah able fo act."

"You de talk God's truth. Now I need fo know dis thing my mom calls 'sexual pleasure.' You able fo tell me?" I asked, still hoping I could get the answer without the act.

He laughed again and said, "Yu de talk poo-mui ways. Na man get pleasure, and woman get pikin."

I stopped cold. Pikin! What was I doing? I hadn't thought about that at all. The last thing I needed was a baby. And in that second the light bulb went on in my confused brain.

"Sorry Joko, du ya, Ah beg, but Ah de craze too too much. I can't do this."

Grabbing his hands, I said it again, "Ah de craze too much. Ah no able fo do dis ting. And yu know someting, Ah de learn jus jus now—lines de in friendship.

"Let wi go," I said. "Ah de know, jus now, Ah de love my sistah Khadi, but Ah de love me more. Ah de live with me time after time, and if Ah no get self respect, Ah no get nothing. Khadi will understand." I knew I would have to think of another way to save her.

"Ah no sabe dis talk, girl love girl." He shook his head again, this time like someone getting rid of a bad smell. "Yu need fo learn sense jus now."

Without saying good-bye he walked away, shoulders straight in the moonlight, his walk slow like a cat on the prowl. "Wi go see," I whispered under my breath, "but after Ah save Khadi.

"Now yu one fine gentleman," I shouted to him as he left. "Yu no make palaver fo me fo my own foolishness. Tank ya, God says, tank ya!"

MY MOM WAS WAITING FOR ME WHEN I GOT home. I felt like a mess, both physically and mentally. She took one look at me and got up and sat on my bed. She tapped the place next to her, so I sat.

Taking my right hand she asked, "It's late. Where have you been? I heard Khadi's group leaves tomorrow. You weren't out making trouble, were you?"

I was too tired to talk, so I just shook my head no as quiet tears from nowhere slipped down my face. Stroking the back of my hand, my mom asked, "Were you with Joko?"

I nodded silently.

A look of alarm crossed my mother's face so I quickly said, "He was a perfect gentleman. And it was all my doing anyway."

"Is this connected to Khadi's going away tomorrow? Did you fight again?"

"Yeah, Mom, to both," I said as I stood, stretched my arms high and yawned like a lion. "But I can't talk about it now. Maybe tomorrow. Definitely not tonight. But it was all about saving Khadi."

"Jodie, wait." She pulled me down next to her again.

"If you want to save Khadi, then you have to let her go. Don't you want to remember the great times you had together instead of a string of little arguments?"

My mom looked out the small barred window and said, "Khadi has no choice but to go, but *you* have a choice. Let the old Khadi go, and be ready to love the new Khadi that comes back."

She swung around to look at me in the flickering light and said, "Jodie, honey, it's up to you to make a choice. Let her go and stay friends, or keep making her angry and never talk again."

I WATCHED A BAT SWOOP THROUGH THE HUT passing in and out of the square of moonlight spilling from the window. He looked slightly blurred through the mosquito net. I finally fell asleep when I admitted to myself that I didn't know what to do—save her or set her free—and wouldn't know until I saw her again.

I got up before sunrise like Khadi and her group and went to find her. I didn't want her to leave with anger between us. She was bent over a bucket, washing her face. She sucked in a handful of water, then ran her finger around the inside of her mouth. I heard her swirl the water around before she spit it out on the ground.

I walked up, with my best fake smile stretched across my face and said, "Aw yusef du dis morning, padi." I threw in "friend" at the end so she would know I wanted peace. She walked around her bucket and took both my hands in one motion.

Bouncing my hands on her upturned palms, she said, "Ah be fine-o." She gave me a hug as Ma Jalloh walked by. "Le wi go jus now," Ma Jalloh told Khadi. "Wi go see," she said to me, moving through the village rounding up girls like the Pied Piper. I watched sadly and madly as they disappeared into the bush. The love we had just shared in those few moments made up my mind for me.

"I have to save her," I whispered out loud.

18

IT WAS TRICKY FINDING THE BREAK THROUGH the broken trees, but after four tries I finally did. Once again I stooped low, beneath branches that crossed the hidden path like fingers intertwined across a gap. Clouds were slowly covering the sun, and the air thickened with humidity. Rain was on the way, Joko had told me—in fact, the first rains of the season. Nodding my head like a pecking chicken, I looked up to avoid getting snagged on a branch, and down to walk without sending crunching signals before me.

As far as I could see there was only one option to save Khadi. It would put me at risk, big time, but it might bring her to her senses. I was determined to get as close as I could so I could jump up and save her if I had to. What if she suddenly changed her mind? Who would help her but me? Who but me would help her escape?

There was no more time to try anything else. For more than an hour, or maybe two, I stooped like an old bent woman, working my way through the thick branches and cobwebs. After an hour of start-and-stop branch-breaking, I could suddenly hear the very faintest traces of music. The drumbeats seemed almost subdued in the heavy, damp air as I worked my way forward through the same creepy, old dead forest.

The music was much more intense than before, and seemed to sink into my bones. Their voices were loud and strong, and the air vibrated with their power. By pushing aside a dangling dry branch, but leaving a lot of twigs that hung in front of my face, I could see Khadi.

They were all sitting in a well-tended clearing in a straight row, biggest to smallest. No bras tonight. Everyone was topless, covered only by a layer of red oil. Strings of colored beads were slung across their chests like bullet bandoleers, drooping down beneath their breasts. Their black skins shimmered as a shaft of sunlight poured through a hole in a cloud and danced around them. The sight took my breath away, for each one looked happier than any person I've ever seen. Especially Khadi.

Her face shining with sweat and joy as she sang and bounced to the beat, her perfect white teeth radiating light and the beads she had strung into her hair tapping together as she swung her head to the pulsing rhythm. She was so beautiful I crept closer.

Ma Mary stood before Salimatu, who suddenly

jumped to her feet. Ma Luba danced in front of the drummer, then threw her head back and ululated with a high-pitched, eerie and yet joyous sound. She did a complicated dance step, which Salimatu copied, while all the other girls clapped and ululated with joy too.

Ma Luba worked her way down the line, passing one girl, going back to another, each joining the dancing line as she bowed in front of them. Khadi had just been chosen when, as her head bobbed left to right, she opened her eyes and somehow, when she stood to join the line, she saw me. She lost the beat immediately and total fear crossed her face. She was the last in the line, standing alone when she lost the beat. Quickly she tried to get back into the swing of things before anyone noticed, but it was too late. Ma Jalloh had seen her face.

Ma Jalloh is a big woman. She sat a head above all the girls and had a clear view. She turned her head like a fish eagle looking for prey. Looking for me.

I pushed down into the ground as far as I could. A branch pierced the skin near my eye, and blood trickled down my cheek. I expected to be clutched by the back of the neck at any time, when suddenly Khadi let loose with a scream that sounded like a person possessed.

The drums picked up speed and everyone gathered around Khadi. Ma Jalloh was at the center of the crowd. The girls were shouting and the drums were beating, and still Khadi kept screaming. Everything was backwards, for Khadi was giving me a chance to escape. Like a lizard I moved backwards, hugging the ground. A sharp branch scraped along my calf, and I felt the blood soak my lapa and cling to my leg. I clenched my jaw as tight as a vice, trying to block out thoughts of snakes and scorpions. Then turning, scared to death, I jumped to my feet and ran like a gecko.

I kept my arms high to protect my eyes from branches, and ran as fast as I could stooped over. My toe started to bleed when I smashed it into a rock, and I heard myself whimpering. The bush seemed to have no beginning and no ending as I thrashed through it.

I didn't try to cover my trail. I was completely lost, just running in a straight line, tearing at branches, hoping to come out in the village. I stopped for a moment to listen if anyone was following, but my own rasping, ragged breath filled the air instead. Looking around for some sign that would show me the way out, I saw only broken branches blocking my way. With a sigh of despair I dropped my head and ran, watching my feet step on lines of traveling ants and sprout little puddles of blood as my right flip-flop broke and I charged on barefoot over pointed sticks. Thrashing and gasping, I finally smelled cooking fires and heard pikins playing. Skirting around the back of the huts to get close to ours, I screeched to a halt like a truck hitting a wall when the snake woman suddenly appeared before me. She looked at my bleeding face and blood-soaked lapa, and the direction I had come from.

Her eyes, just below her snake headband, drilled into me. I hadn't seen her since that day in the market. She rarely came into the village—her juju scared everyone. There was no mistaking her feelings this time—she dun vex pas words. She lifted her little snake bag and angrily shook it in my face. I could hear the bones jangling inside. She waved her other arm like a magician, signaling me to get out of her way. As fast as she could, she headed down the path I'd just come from to tell the women what I had done.

My mom stopped sweeping the ground in front of our hut when I came rushing up. She looked at my bloody face and bleeding leg and said, "Jodie, what's happened? Where have you been?"

I couldn't say anything. I was too scared, and my lungs felt as if they were on fire. My mom hugged me to her, and I felt a horrible guilt surge up my raw throat. I had done everything she had begged me not to, not to mention breaking my promise as well. I knew for sure that I had just spoiled everything we had in Bukama. How could I tell her? I started to cry, and in that same moment the long-awaited rain began to fall.

My mom was pushing me toward the hut when Khadi appeared from the bush. She looked like me—scared and breathless from running. There was terror in her eyes, and her breath heaved in and out. Rain coursed down her face and over her breasts. A string of beads had broken, leaving an empty string dangling.

"Yu need fo leave jus now," she shouted. "Dey dun vex pas words. Time is small small. Dey know wetin you dun."

My mom looked from Khadi to me, and knew right away what I had done. Shock and anger and fear crossed her face. She raced into the hut to grab our passport and moneybag, always hidden beneath her mattress. Over her shoulder she yelled to Khadi, "Go tell Pa Joseph wi need his truck right now. Wi de come."

My mother came running from the hut, our passport bag slung around her neck and her bag of work notes in one hand. Her face was stonelike as she realized that all her hard work, work she loved, was screeching to a halt. She grabbed my arm like a relay runner and, slipping in the mud, we took off.

We tore across the village's main compound that was basically empty. Pa Joseph was moving slowly toward his truck, ignoring the rain falling around him. He saw us running and slipping and sliding, and knew something was very wrong. Rain streamed down our faces so it was hard to see my tears, but he knew something bad had happened.

We all reached his truck together. It was a wreck that my mom had always refused to ride in. She had once told me, "That battery on the front floor, next to the plastic bottle that is the gas tank, is a time bomb. One wild bump and BOOM!" I had already set off my own mini explosion so we scrambled into the cab without a thought for our safety. My mom slammed the door so hard that the rust holding it in place gave way, and the door hung tilted. From the far side of the village we could hear the first of shouting angry voices.

My mom told Pa Joseph, "I give you ten ten dollars if you get this truck going now now."

Two wires dangled from under the dashboard, which the old man held together with shaking hands. Finally the truck lurched to life. We pulled onto the main path through the village and looked behind us. It was getting dark, but I could see women and children running toward our hut. It must have been Ma Jalloh, she was so big, who slipped and crashed to the muddy ground. Everyone stopped to help her up until they saw the truck. Then they all ran toward us, leaving her screaming and shaking her arms in the muddy mess.

Pa Joseph was thinking of the ten dollars, so he gave the truck as much gas as he could. Sliding in the mud, driving with no lights and no wipers, the truck carried us away from the village that had been our home for seven months. The raindrops were like grapes, and water cascaded down the cracked back window.

Water splashed up through the floor and down from

the windshield and in from the vents. All the windows were closed, and a thick fog built up inside the cab.

With our heads together we rubbed a clean spot out on the back window of the truck. The darkness had settled on the ground when a great flash of lightning lit the area behind us. The huts were perfectly outlined, and so were the angry running people. A loud clap of thunder shook the truck.

My mom turned to me with more pain in her face than I'd ever seen before. "You blew it, Jodie. You really blew it."

"I know," was all I could say as the tears streamed down my face. Then under my breath I whispered to a lone figure standing by our hut, "Bye, Khadi. Du ya, Ah beg. Ah be sorry pas words."

epilogue

Khadi finally wrote to me after eight months, and thirteen letters. I held the envelope in my hands trying to feel if she was still my friend. Finally, I opened it. My hands were trembling, so I set the pages on the kitchen table. For a second it struck me as so weird to be looking at a letter from Khadi in the same kitchen I knew before Khadi. With a deep breath I read:

Dear Jodie,

Yu able fo return now. Fo months wi dun talk and talk and tell stories about yu. At first everyone jus talk angry stories about yu, but then one day Ma Jalloh said, "Bemember that girl when she eat leaf sauce and fofo the furst time? The hot pepper be too too much, and the taste too too strange, but she de try to eat and smile and wi de laf and laf."

Then Ma Jenny said, "Ah no forget de day my back ache pas words. That girl dun take my baby and tie her to her own back, giving me the rest Ah be needing. For three days she de come and do like so, and I never forget this kindness."

Soon wi all talking about your good tings and telling funny stories when the shouts turned to smiles and the smiles to silence. Ma Jalloh broke the quiet when she said, "Dis girl want tu bad to be jis like her sistah Khadi. She no bad. Just no respect for when wi say stop. I de miss her and her mama."

Ah lef it like dat, let dem tink so. Why fo say yu wan fo save me, when Ah never wan fo be saved, Jodie. In de quiet Ah finally asked wetin Ah dun wondered and waited seven months to ask, so my mouth was nervous when Ah said, "Can Jodie come back? She only loved us too much. Her willfulness made her foolish pas words."

Ma Jalloh listened to me, slowly nodding her head. Her eyes sparkled as she said, "You go fo write her and say, 'If you no want palaver, noh ple wit pikin.' And tell her if she gets respect for our ways, she able fo cum back. She no get respect wi no need her palaver. Ifn she no yell in de rice field, sneak on the Sande, show disrespect, Ah de say, come."

And she also tank ya fo de lettas to her and the other women. Jodie, Ah be gladdie pas words if yu de cum back. And yu no fo worry, Ah no get grief fo yu actions. All the mothers know that Jodie be the boss of Jodie, and yu do ow yu like. So not to worry, palaver no de fo mi.

And mebbe Ah make yu gladdie when Ah say no daughters of mine go get cut in da future. Jenisa get sick pas words, Jodie, with pain and tears. It too too painful, and fo what? Salimatu de gree wid me, and Njai and a few others. Now wi wait fo de time when wi be in charge, and slow slow make a change. Ah know yu de try to stop me, but wi need fo stop wi selves. Ah tink wi go do so, jus now.

Du ya, Ah beg, na bring yu bodi back dis side quick quick. Joko de gree wit me.

Luv ya sistah,

Khadi

P.S.

Dis be the furst letta Ah de write. Tank ya for teaching me. No beta present de.

I sat and reread the letter many times. Finally I took it to my mom sitting in her office, staring out her window into the garden. She had never quite recovered from how we left Bukama. Just yesterday Felix had told me, "Well Jodie, you can't keep beating yourself up for what you did. You gotta move on."

"And what about my mom? Will she ever forgive me?"

"Sure, if you let her. But first you gotta forgive yourself. It's like your mom told you on your truck ride, 'No condition is permanent.' You, my firend, blew it. Now move on." Thinking of our conversation, I dropped the letter in her lap.

"From Khadi?" she asked.

"Please read it. I need some translating done."

She read it once with a smile that spread across her face as she read down the page. "Let's see," she said, "if you no want palaver, noh ple wit pikin. That roughly means if you don't want trouble then don't play with kids. Know what it really means?"

"Something like if you don't want trouble, don't look for it?"

"Precisely. And what about the respect?"

"I have plenty of respect," I said as I turned to leave the room. I respected her and Khadi for knowing how to accept the lines that can't be crossed between cultures.

"You didn't mention the most important part of the letter. What Khadi says at the end. If it's true then we helped."

Then she did something I hadn't seen in eight months. She threw her head back and laughed. "Jodie, some conditions may take longer than others to change, but ultimately, no condition is permanent." I grabbed my mom and hugged her tight, glad to see her back.

Getting Khadi's letter will let me move on now. It has freed both my mom and me. I don't think I'll rush right back to Africa just yet. But now, when I close my eyes, I see Khadi's face and she's smiling. A smile as bright as an African sky after a cleansing rain. A smile that dazzles the sun.

And I call to her over the ocean and time zones, "Ah de come, sistah, Ah de come one day."

"CLEARLY I NEVER FORGOT"
Words from the author

I lived in Makeni, Sierra Leone, from 1981–83. Makeni is the third largest town in the country, but rarely had electricity, never had running water, and always had snakes. Cobras, puff adders, two-headed asps and mambas, in the house or around it.

Most of the events in this book are based on my experiences there. We traveled around the country, for recreation and for visiting projects that my husband Joe was in charge of for CARE. Makeni is where I started my writing career, with a little portable typewriter facing the wall, and a journal that was with me constantly. Many of the events in the book, like encountering the snake woman in the market, lightning bolts illuminating whole scenes, snakes in the house and horrendous bus rides come straight from the pages of my journals.

Our favorite spot in Sierra Leone was a beach where we would camp, close to a village like Bukama. The name Bukama is made up, but the scenes and descriptions of village life are real. Khadi's physical appearance is based on a beautiful young woman I met up-country, who was the main dancer for her village that was celebrating the opening of a bridge. Khadi's personality is based on the many Sierra Leonean women friends I have, who were forever kind, fun-loving even under difficult conditions and ready to dance at the drop of a hat.

The Secret Society is still a very important element of culture in Sierra Leone. Our home in Makeni backed up to the bush and was close to a Secret Society power spot, so they often danced by, singing, swaying, looking entranced. On one occassion, a Sierra Leonean friend saw me watching them pass. She told me, "They see you they go circumcise you!" I hit the floor faster than plaster falling off a ceiling during an earthquake. Our last year in Sierra Leone was a big initiation/circumcision year. There were drums and dancing and beautiful decorated young women everywhere, strutting their stuff. All those descriptions in the books come from my journals, but the initiations and societies go on even today. Clearly, I never forgot.

C.K.

glossary

(A sample of phrases in order of appearance in book)

Wetin da matta? *(Wet-tin da mat-taw?)*—What's the matter?

da *(dah)*—the

Wi go see. *(We go see.)*—Goodbye / See you later.

Ow di go de go? *(How dee go day go?)*—What's new? / What's happening?

juju *(ju-ju)*—black magic

Ow di bodi? *(How dee bo-dee?)*—How are you?

Lef mi bo! *(Lef me bo!)*—Leave me alone, guy / Go away.

fine-o *(fine-oh)*—fine, good

Ah bi fine-o. *(Ahhh be fine-o)*—I am fine.

Yu de talk na fine-o. *(You day talk nah fine-o.)*—You speak well.

Ow fo do? *(How foe do?)*—What can you do? (Almost always accompanied by a shrug.)

poda-poda *(po dah - po dah)*—public transport, bus, or truck

poo-mui *(poo-mooie)*—foreigner

Cusheo. Wetin wi go do fo una? *(Coo-shay-oh. Wet-tin we go do foe oona?)*—Hello. What can I do for you?

de *(day)*—do

Una tengk ya. *(Oona teng yaw.)*—Thank you.

We yu nem? *(Whey you nem?)*—What's your name?

Ah bi Khadi. *(Ahh be Khaw-dee.)*—I am Khadi.

Le wi tu go. *(Lay we two go.)*—Let's go.

Na. *(Naw.)*—It is / Is it?

Luk we yu de swet! *(Look way you day sweat!)*—Look how sweaty you are!

lapa *(law-paw)*—piece of cloth used for clothing, carrying babies on the back, cushioning head loads

Na bifo fut, na im bien fut de fala. *(Naw beefo foot, naw im bee-in foot day faw-law.)*—The back foot follows the front one.

palaver *(paw-law-ver)*—trouble, problems (Why you want to make trouble?)

fo *(fo)*—for

dis *(dis)*—this

dat *(dat)*—that

Not-a-so? *(Not-ah-so?)*—Isn't that true?

Jisno. *(Jis-now.)*—Just now / Right away.

tink *(tink)*—think

pikin *(peek-in)*—child

Du ya, Ah beg. *(Do yah ahh beg.)*—please

mek *(meck)*—make

Yu de fala makata mi. *(You day faw-law maw-kaw-taw me.)*—You're mocking me / making fun of me.

Ah beg padin. *(Ahh beg paw-din.)*—I beg your pardon.

Na tru. Wi go lan ya. *(Naw true. We go lawn yaw.)*—It's true. We'll teach you.

Sande *(Sawn-de)*—the name of the women's secret society

humbugging *(humbugging)*—bother, irritate

Yu no de gree. *(You no day gree.)*—You don't agree.

sabe *(saw-bay)*—to know or understand something

attal *(at-tall)*—at all

padi *(paw-dee)*—friend

Bad man bete pas emti os. *(Bad man bet-taw pas emti os.)*—A bad man's better than an empty house.

chop *(chop)*—food / meal

Yu need fo siddom lili bit, na rest. *(You need fo sid-dom lil-li bit, naw rest.)*—You need to sit awhile and rest.

Wi no meks pan fomful. *(We no meks pan fum-fol.)*—We aren't fooling around.

Yu tu trangga too much. *(You to trawng-ga too much.)*—You are too stubborn.

wen da sun no komot yet *(wen daw sun no com-ot yet)*—before sunrise

Aw yusef du? *(Awww you-sef do?)*—How are you?

Dey dun vex pas words. *(Day dun vex pas words.)*—They're angry beyond words.

Ah be gladdie. *(Ahh be glaad-di.)*—I'll be so happy.